BREAKING THE RULES

New York Times & *USA Today* Bestselling Author

KENDALL RYAN

Breaking the Rules
Copyright © 2021 Kendall Ryan

Copy Editing by Pam Berehulke

Cover Design and Formatting by Uplifting Author
Services

All rights reserved. No part of this book may be
reproduced or transmitted in any form without written
permission of the author, except by a reviewer who may
quote brief passages for review purposes only.

This book is a work of fiction. Names, characters,
places, and incidents are either the product of the
author's imagination or are used fictitiously.

ABOUT THE BOOK

The bestselling *Hot Jocks* series is back with a brand-new novella. In this much-anticipated return of the hockey team you know and love, you'll see what the guys are up to now and meet the hot new rookie on the team. This series by New York Times bestselling author Kendall Ryan has been called . . .

"PERFECT!" – *Modern Belle*

"A TOTAL, UTTER MUST READ." – *Book Fanatic*

"Delicious and steamy hockey goodness!" – *New York Times* bestselling author Elle Kennedy

"Sexy, smart, fun, and just a damn good time." – *USA Today* bestselling author Avery Flynn

Includes bonus material and deleted scenes from the original series.

CHAPTER ONE

Becca

I f my favorite romantic comedies have taught me anything, it's that once you get married, you live happily ever after. You ride off into the sunset with your Prince Charming and live the good life. Cue the sappy music and roll the credits.

Except my reality is turning out to be so much different.

With a sigh, I smear peanut butter on a slice of bread and wipe a blob of jelly from the counter with a paper towel.

First of all, you should know I married my dream guy—my one-time best friend turned sex tutor, Owen Parrish—and things started off great.

When we got together eight years ago, he was

the starting goaltender for the famed Seattle Ice Hawks hockey team. Life was filled with games and charity galas and private planes. We lived lavishly, completely in love, and enjoyed every stolen moment we could get. Each season was intense, and there was a lot of time away for games all around the US and Canada.

The hockey life was a good life. Whenever he got home from a particularly long trip, we'd basically maul each other with kisses and *I love you*s, and hump like bunnies until it was time for him to leave again.

Summers were spent traveling. At Owen's urging, I left my job in public relations to be able to spend more time with him. We ventured all over the globe, visiting exotic locales like the Seychelles and Portugal, and even Bora-Bora. We ate and drank and napped and, quite frankly, had a lot of sex. Life was blissful.

And yes, I'll admit, sometimes I missed my job, missed my old colleagues and having a purpose, but mostly I was happy. I was living a life most people only dreamed about. It wouldn't have been appropriate to complain about the little things I might have missed. Even if sometimes I felt alone and sad.

Which brings me to the present.

My hair hasn't been washed in four days, my T-shirt is stained with breast milk, and I haven't brushed my teeth yet today, even though it's well past noon.

Worse than that, though? I've kind of lost the ability to care. I'm in survival mode. I'm not sure if you've ever been there, but just getting out of bed in the morning feels like an accomplishment.

And the main reason why I'm so despondent? Well, I'm terrified to tell Owen that I'm pregnant. *Again.* He's been so focused lately, and also so stressed out, I don't want to pile any more worry on him.

Although Owen is still technically on the team at the moment, he's not on the active player roster, which means he's been home with us. Essentially, he's retired. But lately, he's been working with a trainer and has plans to play again rather than retire officially , something I have big, messy mixed feelings about.

I told him I'd support his decision no matter what, but the truth is, I can't imagine us going back to the professional hockey schedule. The training and practices alone are brutal . . . not to mention his traveling for away games.

Owen hasn't even decided yet if a return is possible for him at the age of thirty-five, but he's been training harder than I've ever seen him train. Seven days a week, he's at the gym before I'm even awake most mornings. He's already added fifteen pounds of new muscle and replaced his dad bod with his professional-athlete body.

If he does return to the NHL, I know it will be harder than when he was playing before. For one thing, we'll have four children under the age of six. Everything domestic will fall on me—cooking and cleaning and discipline. Yes, we have a cleaning lady who comes once a week, but she's not here 24/7. I love having my toilets scrubbed and beds made every Tuesday, but there's a lot of life that happens between her visits. I swear my house looks like a tornado passed through it only hours after her visit.

"Bishop! Your lunch is ready!" I call out.

Our six-year-old son, Bishop, is dribbling a basketball down the hallway, even though I've told him at least six thousand times not to do that. The sound bounces off the marble flooring and straight into my brain. I can feel a headache forming behind my eyes. It doesn't help that I've had to give up caffeine.

The twins are crawling around at my feet, probably searching for any crumbs I might have dropped. I need to fix them lunch too.

"Soon, sweetie pies. Soon," I tell them as I carry the sandwich and a plastic cup of milk over to the dining table. "Here you go, buddy."

"Thanks, Mommy," Bishop says, smiling sweetly up at me when he sees I've sliced the sandwich into four tidy squares, just like he likes.

I tousle his hair and lean over to press a kiss to his forehead.

Our son is absolutely adorable. And it's not his fault that I'm overwhelmed. I lean down and give him a sniff. He smells a little like cheese. *Hmm* . . .

I begin a mental list of all the things that need to be done later—dropping off a birthday gift for a friend, returning library books, bathing Bishop and then the twins. Just as I'm giving myself a pep talk, all hell breaks loose.

Bishop drops his sandwich on the floor, and when our naughty goldendoodle puppy snatches it, devouring the thing in two noisy gulps, Bishop begins to cry.

Charli and Bella are next—each of them sobbing along with their older brother. They've always been sympathetic criers. When one of them starts, so does the other, even though half the time, I'm convinced they don't know *why* they're crying.

Emotion wells in my throat. *Keep it together, Becca.*

I can't let myself break down, even if the only thing I want to do is curl into a ball in the center of my bed and cry. For like a thousand years.

Later, I tell myself.

After I secure the twins in their matching high chairs and shush them with kisses, I replace Bishop's sandwich with a new one and shoot our dog a death glare. The twins babble as I fix plates of sliced bananas and avocado for them and then collapse into a dining chair.

I should fix myself something to eat as well, but I'm too exhausted. I'm not sure if it's because I haven't been sleeping well or because of the pregnancy hormones. I'm only about nine weeks along, and I don't recall my other early pregnancies being this difficult.

I'm so tired. All. The. Time.

But this will be the fourth baby my body has grown in six years, so it's *a lot*. Especially on my petite frame. I'm convinced there will be nothing left of my boobs at all by the time I'm done nursing the twins. Which really needs to be any day now. They're ten months old. I need to begin weaning them soon, but it's another chore that I don't want to deal with.

When he's finished with his lunch, I get Bishop settled with a board game, and then wipe sticky globs of banana from between the twins' chubby fingers with baby wipes before I put them down for a nap.

Exhausted, I curl up on the sofa in the living room, thinking I should check my email. Maybe reply to my mom's text. But I'm too tired to move. I let out a huge yawn and have just closed my eyes for a brief nap when I hear the front door open.

"Angel? I'm home," comes Owen's voice from the hallway. "And I have great news."

"Yeah?" I call from the living room.

"Yeah," he says as his footsteps move down the hall. "My agent says Nashville is interested."

My stomach does a weird little flip. It's good news that a team is interested in him, right? That means his dream of coming out of retirement is one step closer.

But *Nashville*? Uprooting our entire lives to move to a city where I have no friends, no family, no connections? And more importantly . . . no childcare help? That thought is terrifying. I'll have four kids soon. Researching new schools, pediatricians, ob-gyn . . . all of it.

Anxiety settles into my chest, making my heart beat faster.

"Becca?" Owen says, his voice closer now.

"That's great," I hear myself say, but my voice sounds far away in my own ears, like I've lost another piece of myself.

Too many more of them, and I fear there will be nothing left of me.

CHAPTER TWO

Owen

"**Y**ou ready, Barnsley?"

Kyle Barnsley is a freckle-faced kid with a bad attitude who would much rather be playing *Minecraft* at home than Little League at the park. He glares at me like I asked him to eat dirt.

Awesome. We're off to a fantastic start.

It's our last game of the season, and I'm thankful for that. When I volunteered to coach, I had no idea what a time commitment this would turn out to be.

I turn the baseball in my hand as I get into position to lob it less than ten feet toward Barnsley's outstretched bat. In moments like these, I have to remind myself that some people aren't cut out for team sports. But then I remember that these *people* are five- and six-year-old children. They aren't cut out for much at all yet.

"Lift your elbows, kid."

It's a lost cause. Kyle lifts his arms way too far over his head, and the weight of the bat tumbles him backward. Soon, he's flat on his ass, crying wet tears all over his freckled face.

"It's okay, man. You'll get it next time."

I nod to Jordie, my catcher for the day. Normally, Grant is my assistant coach, with one of his own kids on the coed team. But he took the weekend off to celebrate his anniversary with Ana a month early in upstate New York, hiring a nanny to take care of their kids.

Becca and I really gotta do that. We're due for a vacation. Somewhere with a warm beach and a great view and no rush to get out of bed. *Christ*, what I would give to spend the day in bed with Becca. But that means we'd need to find a nanny, and fuck if I know where to even start with that. Plus, the twins are probably too young to part with at this point.

There goes that thought.

"These kids suck, dude," Jordie grumbles with

zero remorse after helping Barnsley up and shooing him back to the dugout.

With a stern look, I say, "Watch your attitude around the kids."

He rolls his eyes, still very much the rookie in his maturity level. "Whatever. Lemme pitch or I'm gonna die of boredom."

"Isn't Harper here?"

Nonchalant, he shrugs like I don't know how head over heels he is for his wife.

I glance over at the bleachers, catching Becca's eye. She waves to me with a weak smile on her face.

Ever since I told her about Nashville, she's been distant. And for Becca—sweet, brave, love-of-my-life Becca—that's out of character, and I've felt a weird sense of dread ever since. I don't like her being distant. She's always been my biggest cheerleader, my most vocal supporter. We need to find the time to have an actual conversation.

"Be nice," I say firmly, tossing the ball to Jordie as I turn toward the bleachers. "Fisher, you're up! Parrish, you're on deck."

Bishop is tucked away in the shadowy dugout,

but my kid's face lights up like a damn beacon at the sound of our last name.

He rushes toward me, latching onto my leg. "I want you to pitch!"

"I will, bud. I'll be right back."

I ruffle his dark hair before carefully detaching his strong little hands from my leg. This kid is a force of nature, even at six years old. *He'd be a killer goalie*, I think, grinning at the thought.

Now, where the hell are my other kids?

Becca had dressed them in matching yellow onesies and blue coats this morning when I came home from my workout—our team's colors. A quick scan of the bleachers reveals that Elise has one of the twins in her lap, and Justin is carrying the other, fast asleep on his shoulder.

Elise has been an amazing aunt, filling the role naturally with her big heart and her background as a preschool teacher. I always think that I know Justin better than anyone—he's my best friend, after all—but it still surprises me how good he is with kids. After that one chick from bumfuck nowhere tricked him into thinking he was a dad, I assumed Justin would be scarred for life. But no, he's totally comfortable with kids, great even. They're holding off on having offspring of their own, which I respect. It's hard work.

I jog the rest of the way and sit next to Becca, cracking open a bottle of water from the cooler at her feet. She has a cup of tea hanging limply in her hands while she zones out, staring at the diamond with an empty expression.

"Earth to Becs. You doing okay?" I ask, nudging her knee with mine.

"Yeah," she says quickly. "You?"

I nod. "Just needed a break. Jordie's good with the kids."

We watch Jordie face-palm as the Fisher kid tries to swing the bat like it's a golf club.

"You think?" Harper says, sounding a little skeptical from where she's sitting on the other side of Becca.

I don't blame her. Jordie isn't the most mature of our group. But maybe I'm wrong. Harper and Jordie have been going strong for years now, and I'm sure she knows him better than I do.

Still, the frown on her face gives me pause. Is something up between the two of them? Guess that's something I'll have to investigate later.

"Good enough for Little League," Becca says, and we all chuckle at that.

Soon, Bishop is up, kicking the plate dejectedly and staring back at us on the bleachers as Jordie tries to coax him into swinging.

"That's my cue." I drop a kiss on Becca's head before I head back down.

"I want Daddy," Bishop whines to Jordie, who forces a grin.

"Of course you do. He's the Little League expert, after all. A decade of professional hockey is basically the same thing on a résumé."

"What's a rezz-you-may?"

I pat Jordie on the shoulder and give him a look that says, *Thanks, but fuck off.* And fuck off he does, tossing me the ball and grumbling to himself. Someone's got his panties in a twist.

"You ready, bud?" I give my little guy a smile.

Bishop nods enthusiastically, his face set in the familiar determination of a Parrish at work.

Man, I love this kid.

The first pitch results in a swing and a miss, but that doesn't distract Bishop from the task at hand. I give him a proud grin. It's hard not playing favorites when your son is so damn cool.

"All right, buddy, you got this one. Bend your knees. Just like we practiced."

A simple adjustment later and Bishop taps the bat against the airborne ball, sending it wobbling toward third base like the champ he is. He looks up at me from under his loose baseball cap with a wide, toothy grin.

"Run, man, run!"

With that, he turns and takes off, his little legs pumping as fast as they can, all the way to first base. Our friends holler from the stands like they're witnessing history in the making. Hell, it's the best any of these little goons have done all day.

The kid knows how to make his old man proud, that's for sure.

• • •

The game ends up a well-earned tie.

While parents retrieve their kids, I exchange a firm handshake and a tired look of relief with the other team's coach. There were no meltdowns today, so that's a win in any Little League coach's book.

While Becca and I are packing up our kids in the car, Jordie slaps me on the shoulder. "You seen Harper anywhere? I can't find her."

Becca frowns slightly, which would be invisible to anyone who hasn't memorized her facial expressions like I have. "She said she was going to wait in the car. Headache, I think."

Jordie exhales out of his nose sharply and shakes his head. "Right . . . thanks. See you guys."

"Thanks for your help today, Jordie," I call to his retreating back.

What the fuck is going on with him? Whatever it is, there's nothing I can do about it now, so I shake it off and focus on my family.

After stealing first base like he did, Becca and I agree that Bishop deserves an extra-special treat. There's an ice cream parlor a short drive from the field that we're known to hit up after our games, and this time, Bishop can have all the sprinkles he wants.

As we get situated with our variety of cones and cups of multicolored ice cream on the patio, Becca seems to read my mind.

"What was up with Jordie today?" she asks, pulling the sun guard down over the double stroller where the twins are napping peacefully.

"I was about to ask you the same thing about Harper."

Becca nods in agreement. "Right? They're both acting off. There's some kind of tension between them."

Jordie and Harper met a few years back and got hitched pretty much out of the gate. It was messy, involving a bet made in poor taste, a fake book club, and all the fuckery that comes with dating the coach's daughter.

You heard that right. The rookie and the coach's daughter. But those crazy kids fell in love—the kind meant to last forever. Or so we thought.

"I was hoping I was imagining it."

Becca scrunches her nose, playing with the loose ends of her scarf. "You definitely weren't. I mean, you'd have to be blind to think that nothing's wrong."

There's a harsh edge to her voice that I recognize from the early days of rearing our first kid. Becca was a bundle of stress back then, and I'm sure she's struggling now that her workload has tripled.

Just as I'm reaching out to take her hand, Charli squeals in the front seat of the stroller.

Bishop gulps down the rest of his ice cream in a hurry. He may only be six, but even he knows that life with twins is unpredictable. Sometimes we have to pack up and take off in a hurry, and there was no way he was missing out on the rest of his ice cream.

Becca lets out a little groan as Bella joins in the noise, waking from her slumber with stuttering cries.

Our quiet moment is gone before it really began. Charli is babbling loudly and unhappily, and Bella is growing red in the face with her sympathetic tears.

Becca moves into action, packing everything up. She's a pro by now. We once had to leave a restaurant in the middle of dinner because Charli had blown out her diaper, and Bishop had downed all his chocolate milk in a rush and then thrown up under the table. I swear, you can't make this stuff up. In my defense, I left a *really* nice tip.

Once Becca and I have all the kids calmed

down and packed into the car, we settle in the front seats with heavy sighs. She looks wrecked, resting her head in her hand, propped on an elbow against the window.

I reach across the console and squeeze her knee. "It's not always going to be like this, you know. It's gonna get easier."

She scoffs a little, but her hand finds mine. "I really don't know if that's true."

"I mean it, angel. I know it's a lot, and you handle it all so well. I love you."

Becca cocks her head toward me and smiles, her usual bright blue eyes a muted gray. It's about fifty percent of her smile's usual radiance.

My stomach sinks. *What's happening here?*

That weird tingling feeling inside me is back. I need to get to the bottom of whatever it is that's going on with her.

CHAPTER THREE

Becca

"What are you drawing?" Owen asks our son, pulling up a chair to sit next to him at the kitchen table. A table that will need clearing of all the art supplies scattered over it in less than ten minutes if these goons want any dinner.

Bishop mumbles something unintelligible, concentrating too hard to speak up.

"Belushi? Like the comedian?" Owen chuckles, a little bewildered.

"A beluga," I call out from across the room where I'm stirring a pot of homemade pasta sauce. "He's been into whales lately."

"Ah. Looks good, buddy." Owen rubs our son's hair.

I glance over at the twins, immediately wishing I hadn't. Bella is rubbing a yellow crayon against her cheeks, getting dangerously close to shoving it in her mouth entirely.

"Owen, she's got the crayon in her mouth again."

He leans over and carefully confiscates it. "Hey, hungry, hungry caterpillar. Crayons aren't food."

Bella whines in protest.

"I'm hungry," Bishop says, only contributing to the chaos.

"Your mama's almost done with dinner, bud. You can wait five minutes."

"Ten, at least," I grumble, jogging over to prevent Charli from knocking the whole container of art supplies onto the floor with her surprisingly strong hands.

Bella has managed to get her grubby little fingers on a marker this time, trying to bite off the cap. Owen snags it just in time and shoots me a look that says, *What have we gotten ourselves into?*

Parenthood and all its wonders.

On nights like these, I'm so grateful to have

Owen around to help. He's great with the kids, an honest-to-God fantastic father. But now that we've got three, it takes at minimum two sets of hands to keep them from certain death at all times. Thank goodness the twins aren't walking yet, or else I wouldn't put it past them to toddle into incoming traffic.

Somehow, as if things aren't crazy enough, the fire alarm goes off. I spin around, covering my ears against the noise, which is made louder by the kids screaming along like it's the world's worst song. Smoke is billowing from the oven.

Crap! I left the garlic bread in the oven too long. The slices are as black and hard as hockey pucks.

Owen doesn't need a ladder to turn off the alarm—skyscraper height is a wonderful trait to have in a husband—but unfortunately there's no off switch on a trio of wailing children. And now my sauce is burning. The edges are blackened and the smell is atrocious.

Sighing deeply, I try to shush the twins.

Owen and I decide to nix pasta plans in favor of some simple cheese sandwiches. Neither of us even have the energy to grill them. But there's nothing that Bishop loves more than cheese, and there's nothing his little sisters love more than matching their brother.

Soon, all eyes are miraculously dry and everyone's back on track for a quiet night.

• • •

Long after we put the kids down for the night, tension hangs in the kitchen. Owen scrubs relentlessly at the scorched pot while I nurse a glass of cranberry juice, wishing it were wine.

"When we move to Nashville," he says, "let's hire a personal chef to make all our meals."

Based on the half smirk he gives me, I can tell that he's joking. Still, it kind of stings.

"I'm trying my best, okay?"

He pauses, his hands at rest as his dumb man-brain catches up with his words.

When he meets my eyes, his are full of contrition. "I'm sorry, angel. I didn't mean it like that. You're doing great."

I nod, accepting his apology. But something is eating away at me, and I feel like if I don't say it right now, I'll end up like the swiss cheese I put on the kids' sandwiches—kinda nutty and full of holes.

"Nashville is a big move," I say carefully. "Away from our friends. Our support system. Your parents. Bishop's school."

"True. But you've said yourself that we're due for a change. Nashville could be that change."

I think back on a late-night conversation we had over wine maybe two days before I found out about baby number four.

I guess I did say that, didn't I? Oh, how naive that Becca was.

"I just don't know if it's the right time."

"Oh, come on. What do you have against Nashville, Becs? I know you don't like country music, but I promise it's not all—"

"Owen, I'm pregnant, okay?"

"You're . . ." He half turns to me with a confused smile on his face, as if he's waiting for me to finish the joke.

No punch line this time, buster. Just a punch-to-the-gut reality check.

Owen's smile slowly fades. When all I do is

blink at him, he turns off the faucet and hangs his head, staring at the suds.

My heart is crawling up my throat, pounding painfully in my ears. I need him to say something. *Say anything.*

"We weren't even trying," he says, his voice deep.

And just like that, my heart plummets. I don't know what exactly I wanted him to say, but that wasn't it.

I clear my throat, trying to dislodge the lump there. "I know. The doctor said that the pill isn't one hundred percent effective. So there was always a chance."

"How long have you known?"

"About a week."

"How are you feeling?"

"Physically? I'm okay."

"Good. That's good. I'm . . . gonna go for a run," he says suddenly, shooting me a sideways glance that has all of my insecurities doing the rumba.

"But the dishes—"

"I'll finish them in the morning. Let's talk about this later."

Owen drops a kiss on my head, just like he always does, but I barely feel it. I listen halfheartedly as he rushes upstairs, opening and closing drawers to change into his running clothes. He's down the stairs and out the door in less than two minutes.

"Be safe," I call out.

"I will," he calls from the foyer.

The door closes behind him, and all is quiet on the Parrish front. I lean back in my chair, resting my hand on my belly.

That was the hard part. I told my husband that we're expecting our fourth child. Now he knows, even if his reaction wasn't all puppies and roses. I don't blame him. I also told him I'm not so sure about his plans for Nashville.

I remember Owen's reaction when we found out about Bishop. He was over the moon, and so protective. The memory feels distant, like it's someone else's. I remember too what he said when I told him about the twins. He'd lifted me into his arms and kissed me.

I try not to think too hard about how, this time,

his first impulse was to run.

CHAPTER FOUR

Becca

"**D**on't!"

When Bishop screeches at the top of his lungs, I pivot in the patio chair to gauge whether it's a happy screech or a bad screech. With a quick scan of Ana's yard, I spot Hunter chasing Bishop around the petunia bed, little Bobbie on their heels.

Okay, definitely a happy screech. Carry on, gremlins.

My son may be causing a ruckus, but my girls are more than happy to sit back and relax with us ladies. Elise bounces Charli on her knee while I keep Bella gleefully occupied with a teething ring. Meanwhile, Harper avoids too much contact with the little ones, but that's not unusual.

Brunch with my girlfriends has become more

and more difficult over the years with Ana and me juggling full-time motherhood responsibilities. Harper and Elise have been great about it, agreeing to meet at one of our homes rather than the handful of cute brunch spots we used to frequent. These days, Ana and I alternate hosting every month, and it works well enough when the kids are on good behavior. Fewer mimosas, more "Mommy this" and "Mommy that."

"I don't know how you two do it," Harper says between bites of Ana's homemade quiche.

"It helps for them to have built-in friends." Ana giggles, shooting me a wink. "They're old enough to entertain themselves for the most part. Hunter adores Bishop."

"Ditto," I say, wearing the most cheerful smile I've managed all week.

We always go around the table and talk about our husbands—how they're doing this season, what date nights have looked like recently, what's been causing any stress at home (if anything).

But when it's my turn, I immediately turn to Harper. "How are things with Jordie?"

Luckily for me, no one calls me out for avoiding the same question about Owen. The only evidence I have that he came home last night is the pile of running clothes in the hamper. He was gone again before I opened my eyes. When he said we'd talk about baby number four later, I guess he really meant *later*.

"Jordie? He's . . . fine. He's always fine. But I'm . . . Well, long story short, the honeymoon period is over and our marriage might be next."

Elise and I share a quick knowing look. This is just like Harper, ready to fire off a bold statement when she's on the defensive.

Ana, ever the peacekeeper, gives Harper a soft smile. "What makes you think that?"

"I'm pregnant."

Are you kidding me? Is my whole life an echo chamber? I'm half waiting for 2003 Ashton Kutcher to jump out of the bushes with a full camera crew and yell, *You've been punk'd!*

Then Harper says, "With twins," and I nearly burst into laughter. What are the chances?

"Oh my God, Harper! Congratulations!" Elise squeals, so enviably out of touch with no kids of her own.

Harper shakes her head in response, like she's

turning down an offer for seconds. "Thank you, but . . . I just don't think Jordie can handle twins. I don't even know if I can."

"Have you told him?" Ana asks gently, wrapping one of Harper's hands in her own.

She's so effortlessly maternal. God, I wish I was like that.

"Not yet. I guess I'm kind of scared to."

I want to tackle Harper with a hug and say, *Me too. I'm pregnant too, and I don't know what to do either! I feel what you feel!*

But before I can say anything, she mumbles, "No offense, Becs, but I've seen how hard it is on you and Owen, having twins."

"None taken. It is hard."

Maybe it's not what she wants to hear, but it's the truth. I wish someone would have told me how difficult it would be. Maybe I wouldn't be so hard on myself now.

"And if it could get any better," Harper says, "they're due in the spring, right around the play-offs."

We all nod sympathetically. Each of us knows

firsthand how tunnel-visioned our guys can be during playoffs. Owen does a good job of hiding it, but I can see it in small ways every year—he's less talkative, adheres to a stricter diet, and a few more gray hairs seem to sprout from his temples.

"I'm scared to tell him," Harper says.

Ana squeezes her hand. "I get that. Having kids is the craziest thing I've ever done. Half the time I feel like I'm one tantrum away from passing them off to the nanny for good."

We all burst into giggles at that. It's only funny because Ana would literally never part from her kids. They're her whole world.

I can relate, but maybe I'm a little less well-adjusted about it all. Maybe I want a slice of the world just for myself, you know?

"Do you want to have kids?" I ask, since no one else has.

Harper looks down at her belly, rubbing a hand over her high-waisted leggings. "Yeah, I do."

"Then he will too. Jordie loves you so much, Harp. He may be a little thrown at first, but he'll catch up and support you through it. He's gonna be an awesome dad. I promise."

"Was that how Owen reacted when you told him about your last pregnancy?" she asks, genuinely curious.

Little does she know how recent that conversation actually was.

"Yup," I choke out, refusing to eat my own words. Owen had better catch the hell up. Baby number four on my mind, I turn to Ana and ask, "Do you think you'll have any more kids?"

"No way," she says, laughing with wide, honest eyes. "My hands are full as it is."

I'm silently stewing when Ana returns the question.

"Um, well . . . *surprise*." I force my mouth into a smile and place a hand on my belly.

I think by their reactions, my answer wasn't the one they anticipated. This time, Elise holds off on the congratulations.

"Wait, seriously?" she asks.

I nod sheepishly. I didn't mean to hijack this conversation. "We weren't trying or anything. It kind of just happened. It was a big surprise for both of us."

"A happy surprise?" Ana asks, testing the waters.

I catch Harper's eye, and it's like looking in a mirror. "Um, not an *unhappy* one. Just . . . complicated. Three kids are a party, you know? Four are a circus. Owen freaked a little."

"He's probably just recalibrating," Ana says. "Men take longer to process big life changes."

Elise frowns, wrapping an arm around me and giving me a tight half hug. "He'll come around for sure. My brother is an idiot for making you feel insecure like this."

"But with retirement, he'll be around even more than usual. It might be fun. A kid on each arm. That's kinda hot," Ana says with a ticklish poke to my side.

"He, uh, isn't retiring." That had been the plan when this season and his current contract ended. But things change. "Actually, he's in talks with Nashville right now."

"Nashville?" Harper asks, her nose wrinkling in disgust. "What the hell is in Nashville?"

"Only the third best team in the nation."

"He wants you guys to up and move to Nashville?"

I nod, and just like that, the group of women who have so graciously tried to lift my spirits are down on my level.

"He can't just ask you to . . ." Elise trails off, clearly perplexed that her brother would put me in this situation.

Me too, Elise.

"To be fair, I only told him last night. So don't crucify your brother yet."

Ana seems at a loss of words when she finally says, "You're right. That is complicated."

A silence falls around us. Still, their presence is a comfort in itself.

Who else can relate to my specific troubles? Of all the women I know, these are the few who understand that NHL doesn't mean National Hockey League. It means No Home Life—because our husbands' travel schedule during the season has them playing away games in cities around the country several nights a week.

CHAPTER FIVE

Owen

"**K**eep it open," Grant tells the waitress, holding out his credit card and motioning to the rest of us at the table. "Drinks are on me tonight, fellas."

"Sure thing. Two lagers and three IPAs coming right up." She tucks the card into her notepad, taking extra care to shoot our rookie extraordinaire Preston a smile and a wink. "I'll be right back, handsome."

Preston doesn't so much as look at her, let alone smile back.

"That's it," Jordie says with a snicker. "We're calling you Handsome from now on."

Our team captain has always had a soft spot

for rookies, so it was no surprise that Grant invited the new kid out for drinks. Preston got called up from the minor affiliate team and has been training with the Ice Hawks for a few weeks, but I can't say I really know the guy. As far as I can tell, he doesn't have much of a personality. He's quiet, focused, and unproblematic. Hell, that's probably why Grant likes him.

Jordie's still chuckling when the waitress returns with our beers.

"To the new season!" Grant lifts his beer and we all follow suit, clinking our pint glasses together and spilling onto the plastic menus.

It isn't the fanciest joint in town, but any old run-of-the-mill brewpub would have done the job after a long week of practice. It's weird being out of the swing of things, but I'm grateful that the guys still think to include me, even if I'm no longer on the active team roster.

"And to the new kid," Justin says, clapping Preston on the shoulder.

"To Handsome!"

Preston gives us a half smile and mutters a thank-you before guzzling down half his drink in record time. Wiping his mouth with the back of his hand, he asks, "Anyone want another?"

Grant shoots him a critical look. "Slow down, son. It's not a competition."

With a shrug, Preston heads for the bar, and I clock a group of women ogling him on the way. When one of them shoots her shot with a sultry little wave of her fingers, he brushes her off without a glance.

I can't say I miss that. I never grasped how marriage would change these nights out with the guys until I had an actual ring on my finger. Now that most of the team is off the market, we don't get nearly as much female attention as we used to when we were single. Speaking for myself, I prefer it this way.

"Missing the glory days?" Jordie asks, catching me watching the rookie.

"Don't say that," Justin grumbles. "I already feel old as shit."

"That's 'cause you are. All of you. Bunch of old farts if I ever saw any."

I scoff. "Yeah? Well, this old fart's in talks with Nashville."

Jordie's mouth drops open. "No shit?"

"No shit."

Grant beams with pride. "That's great, Parrish. I'm happy for you."

"Another for number twenty-two!" Justin calls out, waving down the waitress.

"It's not official yet, so hold the damn parade."

There's a commotion at the bar, and we turn to see Preston staring down at what looks like a fruity cocktail spilled all over his front. Some chick with long blond hair presses napkins against his wet shirt, clearly feeling him up under the guise of helping.

"Oh my God, I'm so sorry," the girl says, the empty glass in her hand evidence of a drunken collision. "I didn't even see you there."

"That's a fat lie," Justin says under his breath.

He's right. I can count on two hands how many times some random woman "accidentally" spilled her drink on me to get my attention. Plus, Preston is like six foot four and huge. She saw him, all right.

"It's fine," Preston grunts.

"I'll order you another," she says, waving to the bartender, but Preston is already pushing past her toward the front door, leaving her where she stands.

She turns and hisses, "Fucking jerk!" before storming off toward the bathrooms, a slew of equally drunk friends trailing behind her.

Grant and I exchange a look. Standing from the table, I intercept Preston before he's out the door.

"Relax, rookie. If you're gonna play in the big leagues, you gotta let them flirt. Rumors of asshole behavior spread like STDs around here. No need to take off after one spilled drink."

"Asshole behavior? I'm not the—" He cuts himself off when he notices all the eyes in the room on him. "I'm not leaving. I've got a spare shirt in the car."

I grin. "Go change. I'll buy your next beer."

With a nod, he heads out the door.

"We don't have to haze the newbies with all these puck bunnies around. They do it for us," Justin mutters into his pint glass.

"What's the news on Nashville?" Grant asks, redirecting the conversation.

I sit back down. "They're interested. My agent's

waiting to hear back from me on my decision.”

“So, if you say yes, what’s next?”

“I guess I move to Nashville.”

Grant furrows his brow. “Becca and the kids too?”

“I sure as hell hope so. I’ve gotta talk to Becs more. Make sure we’re on the same page and all that.”

Jordie leans forward, drama junkie that he is. “Why wouldn’t you be on the same page?”

“I mean, we are. She’s supportive and all, but . . .”

“But?”

I scratch the back of my head, feeling tired already. I can’t imagine how my wife must be feeling. “We’re expecting.”

“Wait, another?” Justin asks, surprise written all over his face.

I nod in response. I’m still processing the news myself.

Jordie chokes out an incredulous laugh. “Ding, ding, ding! Round four?”

Grant reaches across the table to squeeze my shoulder. "Congratulations, man. That's amazing."

"Thanks. You guys responded to the news a hell of a lot better than I did."

"How's Becca doing?" Grant asks.

I stare into my beer. "She's okay."

Grant narrows his eyes, smelling bullshit like it's caked on my face. "And you?"

I try out my best nonchalant shrug, but if I'm being honest, fuck if I know. We're losing our minds with three kids already. Add a fourth to the mix, and I have no idea how I'm supposed to pursue my career, knowing I'd be leaving Becca at home, so outnumbered. I have enough guilt about playing again already.

If I had the balls, I'd admit the truth to myself. My hockey career is over. I had a solid run, a fucking fantastic one, even. But shit happens, right? Life changes and you move on, left with only memories of those good times.

Tonight, I don't have the balls. Instead, I talk Nashville stats with the guys and grab Preston that beer. I stay out late and don't look at the clock.

For a little while longer, I let myself pretend I

can reconcile my dreams with my reality.

CHAPTER SIX

Becca

I'm starting to think the universe has a personal vendetta against me.

Bishop woke us up at the ass-crack of dawn on a weekend morning, then had a tantrum until I agreed to let him watch cartoons in the den. Around seven, the twins wouldn't take the bottle, still refusing to eat anything that doesn't come straight from my nipple. *Then*, around eight, I puked in the kitchen sink.

Just your average Saturday morning, right?

I'm dozing on the couch when Owen comes back from his morning run. He usually takes a longer route, so I'm a little startled when he returns in under an hour.

"Didn't mean to scare you," he says, kicking off his shoes.

"You just surprised me. Is it supposed to rain or something?"

"No. I just couldn't stop thinking. We should talk."

Ah. The long-awaited *later* has finally arrived. "Okay."

My stomach feels unsettled, and I really hope I don't throw up again. He sits down next to me, and a whiff of his masculine scent hits my nose.

God, I miss going on runs with him. Ever since the pregnancies . . . well, let's just say my body isn't quite the same. I'm not the spry, bouncy twenty-something I used to be. Plus, running makes me pee my pants.

Owen takes my hand in his, caressing his thumb over my knuckles, and I feel tears forming behind my eyes already. "How are you feeling?"

"Not great. Nauseated and tired."

He nods. "Want some mint tea? Some toast?"

My heart swells. When I was pregnant with the twins, I had awful morning sickness. Like *head glued to the toilet all morning* sickness. On those hellish days, Owen would always brew me some tea and make me breakfast, something simple to settle my stomach.

"That sounds perfect." I offer him a weak smile.

When Owen comes back from the kitchen, a steaming mug in one hand and a plate of peanut butter toast and sliced bananas in the other, the tears begin to fall.

He's used to the pregnancy hormones, so he doesn't badger me with questions like *what's the matter?* or *did I do something wrong?* like he did when Bishop was still in my belly. Instead, he just lets me cry, wiping tears from my cheeks with his thumbs and wrapping me in his impossibly strong arms.

"It's gonna be okay," he murmurs over and over.

"I don't know. I don't know if it is gonna be okay. I'm not sure if I'm ready for this again. I can't imagine having a newborn. I've barely begun weaning the twins off breast milk, and I have no idea how I'm going to nurse another kid. My boobs are pretty much deflated balloons at this point, and—"

"Your boobs are not deflated balloons. I love your boobs." As if to prove his point, Owen cups one in his big hand.

I wince involuntarily. "Don't, Owen. They're sensitive."

He removes his hand and places it on his knee—safer territory. "I'm sorry, Becs. I'm sorry about everything. I'm sorry that I can't seem to do anything right lately. I'm sorry I don't have the right words or the right reactions. Fuck, I'm sorry that my sperm is so *hell-bent* on finding its way into your eggs."

A wet giggle escapes my lips. "Yeah, you have pretty forward sperm for a goalie."

Owen laughs, deep in his chest, before pressing a warm kiss to the crown of my head. "I mean it. I'm sorry for all of it. Please tell me how to fix this. I need you back. I need your smile. I need you to be okay."

His arms tighten around me, enveloping me in profound love.

As much as I want to feel comforted, there's an emptiness inside me that swallows his sweet words, leaving me hollow. "I don't think you can fix it. This is just our life."

A heavy silence falls over us. I watch the steam rise from my cup of tea, wishing I could feel as light as evaporated water. My eyelids flutter closed, and a restless half sleep comes over me.

Soon, a shrill cry from upstairs jolts me awake, and doubles in volume almost instantly. I guess the twins are up from their morning nap.

"I've got them. Get some rest." Owen kisses me softly on the lips before rising from the couch. His eyes are deeply concerned when I get up anyway and follow him to the staircase. "Becca . . ."

"I'm fine. You'll need the backup," I say with a sigh, waving off his worry.

That's the thing about twins. Two sets of hands are kind of required. So I follow him up the stairs.

CHAPTER SEVEN

Owen

"You're making the right call."

Man, did I need to hear those words today.

Grant's voice is gruff over the phone, but comforting in that *wise old man* way he's always managed to pull off without actually being old at all. After spending the last hour arguing with my agent, I knew our team captain would be the next person I needed to call with the news.

I release a slow sigh and rub one hand over the back of my neck. "Thanks, man. I know I am."

Next, I call my best friend, Justin, then Jordie and a few other members of the team. It takes me half the morning, but it's necessary. With each call, I feel more and more confident in my decision.

When I'm done, the twins are down for a nap and Bishop is bouncing a basketball in the yard. I find Becca in the kitchen, loading the dishwasher. She's conveniently turned away, so it gives me a moment to scope out the right spot to display the ornately wrapped gift basket in my arms without her seeing.

I have Elise to thank for the quick tutorial on basket presentation. I'm careful to avoid the droplets of red sauce scattered across the counter, grabbing a damp cloth to wipe them away.

"SpaghettiOs?" I ask.

"Yep. Bishop's on a kick. Loves 'em."

"Like father, like son."

Becca chuckles softly. "Are you done with your work stuff?"

"I'm all yours."

She turns to give me a smile and then does a double-take when she sees the massive gift basket taking up space on the counter. Turning off the faucet, she looks at me like I've sprouted tentacles out of my ears. "It's not our anniversary."

"Doesn't have to be our anniversary for me to pamper my wife."

Her mouth curls into an irresistible grin when I say *my wife*. All these years later, she still loves hearing it, almost as much as I love saying it.

"Uh-huh . . . Should I open it?"

"Go ahead."

With an excited glint in her eyes, Becca pulls away the ribbons. Her greedy hands turn hesitant as she begins to lift mounds of light pink terrycloth out and onto the counter. "Robes?"

"Keep going."

Narrowing her eyes at me in suspicion, she digs a little deeper and finds a cream-colored envelope and a matching box nestled in the bottom.

"Ooh, layers? So mysterious."

"Open the envelope first."

"Yes, sir."

Her sexy little smirk has me thinking all sorts of dirty things on a Sunday afternoon.

Peeling open the envelope, she pulls out a letter. "*Dear Becca . . .*"

"Don't read it out loud," I grunt, half out of embarrassment and half because I'd rather just watch her face as she reads. In any case, I know what it says by heart.

With a smile, she scans the letter.

> *Dear Becca,*
>
> *This morning, I called my agent to tell him that I wouldn't be returning to the NHL. The guys know too. I swore them to silence so that I could be the first to tell you.*

Becca's eyes meet mine over the paper. I nod, silently encouraging her to read on.

> *Here's the thing. I got a better offer. The hours are grueling, and I don't get paid in the traditional sense. But I love it. Being a good dad is a full-time job. The best full-time job I've ever had, actually. My favorite part of the day isn't spent on the ice. It's when I'm home with you and our kids. Having our fourth child is gonna require all hands on deck—a commitment I'm ready to make. I'm sorry it took me a while to realize that.*

This time when her eyes meet mine, they're

glossy with tears. She blinks twice and lowers her gaze to the paper.

> *I know I can't buy your forgiveness. Still, I hope you'll consider this gift basket the kickoff of a long apology tour. You once said pink suits me—and it certainly suits you—so I bought us matching robes to take on our week-long getaway right here in Seattle. There's a name for that, but I can't remember what it is right now. Anyway, it's all planned out, so you have nothing to worry about. The hotel spa is no Number One Foot, but I think we'll have fun.*

Letter writing is weird. I'm not good at it, but it seemed like the better alternative to trying to say all of this out loud without fucking it up. How do I end this thing? I guess I'll wrap up with what's important.

> *I love you, Becca Parrish, and I always, always will.*

> *Yours forever,*

> *Owen*

Tears are freely streaming down her cheeks now, but she's never looked more beautiful.

Pulling my wife into my arms, I cradle her against my chest, rocking us back and forth. She holds on for dear life, like she's been containing her tears all this time and the floodgates finally broke.

"—cation," she says with a hiccup.

"What did you say?" I ask, tilting her chin up so that our eyes meet.

"It's called a staycation," she whimpers before smooshing her face back against my hoodie, now wet with her tears.

I chuckle and press a kiss to the top of her head. "There's more on the back," I whisper, and Becca immediately grabs the letter and flips it over with the excitement of a little kid discovering one last hidden present under the Christmas tree.

> *P.S. As for the box . . . I got you the new model. Can't wait to watch you use it.*

For a moment, Becca stares blankly at the words. Then the box. Then the words. I swear, I can actually *hear* when it finally clicks.

With tentative hands, she opens the box to reveal a brand-new toy, not unlike the first one I got her way back when. This particular vibrator has even more features and settings that I know she'll appreciate.

Full brag, I'm kind of the expert on all that pleasures Becca. I am her husband, after all.

Soon, laughter has replaced the tears, and Becca is wrapping her arms around my neck to kiss me sweetly on the lips. With her nails running through my hair, she sucks on my lower lip before opening her hot, insistent mouth to my tongue.

I spin her against the counter, pressing her ass into the marble and nudging my knee between her legs. I'm about to lift her up when she pulls back with a wet pop of our lips.

"Wait, what about a babysitter?"

"Your mom is staying with the kids for the whole week."

"Seriously? When is she getting here?"

I glance at the clock overhead. "Any minute."

Becca yelps when I duck my head down to nibble on her neck. "Owen! I have to put the vibrator away before my mom sees it!"

Now, there's a sentence I never thought I'd hear . . .

I growl into her ear, closing my eyes to truly savor the moment. "Becca Parrish, you are fulfilling all of my high-school fantasies, and you don't even know it."

She giggles at that, squealing when I slide my hands down her waist and around her ass, lifting her easily onto the counter to press against her with my now raging hard-on. Heat radiates from between her legs, and her eyes darken at the feel of my cock straining against my joggers.

Immediately, we're locked in another breathless kiss, tangled up like we're teenagers. I caress her breasts gently, remembering how tender they must be, and then it hits me.

Oh fuck.

"What's wrong?" Becca asks when I pull away, those big blue eyes wide with confusion.

I sigh, smoothing wild strands of her hair back from her face. "I forgot that you're still nursing."

She blinks. "Oh yeah."

I plant my hands on the counter, dropping my head to her shoulder in defeat. Some "good dad" I am. I planned an entire getaway trip for my wife and didn't consider the fact that her boobs have to stay in the general proximity of our twins.

I guess we won't be far. We could try to come back for meal times. But with how often the twins eat, it might be safer to reschedule. Should we try to bring them with us? Then Bishop will feel left out and we'd have to bring the whole family, which entirely defeats the purpose of a *getaway*.

A soft hand brushes my jaw, lifting my face.

"I have to wean them anyway," she says soothingly. "I've already started bottling breast milk. There's gotta be at least four days' worth in the freezer. I can pump some more before we leave, and that'll give us another half day. The timing is honestly kind of perfect."

"You sure?"

"Yes."

With that, she surges forward, capturing my lips in another searing kiss. I rake my fingers through her hair, grasping a handful at the back of her head and pulling just hard enough to elicit a moan.

I drag long, hot kisses down her neck and over her collarbones, only stopping to say, "I'm sorry,

Becs. I'm sorry for—"

Becca lifts my face once again, this time to give me the stern look she's mastered as a mother of three, soon to be four. "Hey. I love you, Owen Parrish. Now shut up and kiss me."

And I do.

CHAPTER EIGHT

Becca

Five months later

"Three . . . two . . . one . . ."

The buzzer sounds overhead, and the crowd erupts into a roaring celebration. In one of the most nail-biting games of the season, the Seattle Ice Hawks reign victorious yet again with only seconds to spare on the clock. It's the kind of night that burns into your memory—the kind you'll look back on with a knowing smile and tell your grandkids about.

Screeching with excitement, the girls and I jump to our feet. Well, Ana and Elise jump. Harper and I have to take a gentler approach with our seven-month-pregnant bellies. And even though my back aches from sitting in the hard plastic chair, absolutely nothing can stop me from screaming my head off and punching a fistful of half-eaten soft pretzel in the air.

Tonight has been like every other game in so many ways—expert plays, close calls, breath-stopping action. But this particular game was different in one exceptional way: Owen Parrish was back on the ice.

When we got the call from Coach Dodd asking Owen to sub in as goalie, there was no question. He was on the relief list, and he immediately said yes. For the first time since his retirement, I got to see that familiar fire rekindle behind my husband's eyes. Once again, he would play with the team he'd spent his whole career with, the guys who are his friends. His family.

"Par-rish . . . Par-rish . . . Par-rish . . . Par-rish . . ."

As the crowd chants his name, I just about explode with joy. The guys swarm Owen on the ice, crowding around him with a brotherly love so intense that I can feel it from fifty yards away. I blink back tears as Harper hooks her arm into mine and rests her head on my shoulder.

"This is amazing." I sigh wetly, and somehow

over the noise, she hears me.

"I know. You must be so proud!"

Proud doesn't even begin to cover it.

I watch as the team bumps their helmets against Owen's, and pat him on the back with gloved hands. They have so much love and respect for this man—just like I do.

The four of us make our way down from our third-row seats to meet our husbands at the edge of the ice. One by one, they greet us, red-faced and beaming with that post-game high I've missed so much.

Justin takes Elise's hands and kisses them one by one like the prince and princess they are. Ana gives Grant a wave, and he grins back. Meanwhile, Jordie takes a knee to give a quick play-by-play of the game to Harper's belly—twice the size of mine since she's expecting double the trouble. And to think she was ever worried about him rising to the challenge of fatherhood.

Finally, I meet Owen's eyes, brighter than I've seen them in months. Don't get me wrong, Owen loves being a fulltime dad. But going cold turkey on the hockey lifestyle was definitely taking a mental and physical toll on him.

Seeing him so happy in his element again, it occurs to me that maybe this is all he needed—one more time to experience that rush of adrenaline, to hear the crowd of fans chant his name. One more "W" to truly feel like his career is complete.

Owen wraps me in a breathless hug. I cling to him, inhaling the masculine scent of hard work that's paid off.

When I feel like I can't squeeze him any tighter, I lean back and ask, "Did you see the goalie out there?"

Owen smirks, catching on. "No, how'd he do?"

"Not bad."

He scoffs. "Not bad?"

I loop my arms around his neck and pull him down for a kiss. "Not bad at all."

"Nice work out there, man," one of the newer guys says, clapping Owen on the shoulder as he passes by. I think his name is Preston. "Looking forward to next time."

"Same, man. You're killing it out there. I'll see you later?"

"Nah, I gotta get home. You two have a great

night." With a distant look in his eyes, the rookie disappears toward the dressing room.

"Next time?" I ask, arching an eyebrow.

A devilish grin spreads across Owen's face like butter on bread. "It's a long shot, I'm sure, but hey, you never know."

EPILOGUE

Owen

Six months later

"You boys have fun!" Becca calls over her shoulder, blowing me a kiss and following the other hockey wives out the front door.

Our house was the rendezvous spot for their evening plans—dinner at the new Asian fusion restaurant in the neighborhood, followed by some cheesy chick flick at the historic movie theater. Knowing them as well as we do, we know they'll probably stop for midnight margaritas at their favorite Mexican spot before they call us for a ride. Years of this, and we've got Girls' Night down to a science.

The door clicks shut, leaving Grant, Justin, Jordie, and me to watch the tiny humans for the next several hours. There are eight of them between the four of us, so we're vastly outnumbered.

Jordie waits until the coast is clear before launching back into his *cloth versus disposable diaper* tirade. "Anyway, like I was saying—"

Before he can really get into it, the door swings back open and Harper pokes her head in to yell, "Jordie! Don't forget to change the girls' diapers!"

The door closes again and Jordie rolls his eyes, gesturing to the twins on the diaper-changing pad where he's already begun operations. "She says this as if I can't smell them."

Ava and Ella are only four months old—roughly the same age as my little Colson. It's the time when babies will smile and laugh at pretty much anything, especially their dad's funny faces as he changes their rank-ass diapers.

I get some sick satisfaction watching someone else deal with the reality of twins. Double the cute, double the crap. The serendipity of it all still gets to me sometimes. I guess twins run in the NHL family.

"Look, I've done the research, and cloth diapers are massively better for the environment," Jordie says. "Our landfills are at *minimum* two percent used diapers."

"Maybe so, but disposables are massively better for my sanity," I shoot back. "I'm not spending hours every day shoveling sh—I mean, *crap* out of three kids' worth of glorified napkins."

I look down at Colson, the little guy sound asleep in my arms. He had a long day, staring at his older siblings and having a complete meltdown whenever they left the room or even his line of sight. The twins are upstairs taking a nap too, thanks to Becca. It's a blessing for more than one reason. Since they're bipedal now, all our girls want to do is poke and pull at their new baby dolls, Ava and Ella.

Reluctantly, I turn my attention back to Jordie, who is fastening each cloth diaper with some kind of snapping contraption.

He shakes his head, sighing as he says, "It's not that bad, man. You gotta at least give it a shot."

Jordie looks to Grant for help, who merely tips his beer back and says, "We used disposable."

I lift my own beer in grateful acknowledgment.

"Justin?" Jordie gives him a pleading look.

"I don't think I get an opinion in this particular

field," Justin says with a shrug, blissfully childless.

Sometimes I envy the guy. But then I remember that having kids was the best decision I've ever made, and I wouldn't change a thing about that.

"You guys just lack imagination. I'm telling you, the pros are undeniable. Cloth is cheaper in the long run. And it's better for sensitive skin." He tips his head down, his voice suddenly more lyrical and goofier. "Isn't that right, Ava? Ella?"

The girls coo in response, squirming happily in their fresh diapers.

Before I can push back with why I think the whole cause is pointless and unsanitary, Bishop tears into the house from outside. *Damn*. I thought we'd have him and Grant's kids occupied with chalk on the patio for a little while longer.

"Dad! Dad! Can we play with the bikes now?"

"Yo, Bishop!" Jordie intercepts my son, offering him a high five. "What do you think, man? You wanna save the planet?"

"Yeah!"

I watch as my son smacks Jordie's open hand in a high five that could be heard around the world.

"Jesus," Jordie mutters with a wince, flexing his bright red hand.

Atta boy.

As Bishop takes a deep breath, I sit back in my chair, kicking my legs out. Jordie has no idea what's about to hit him.

"Actually, I think a lot about saving the trees—like the big ones *and* the little ones. All the flowers too. It's super, super important. Oh, and the ozone too because the ozone is up in the sky and it keeps us from burning up by, um, by blocking the sun and stuff. It's part of the *atmospear*, but like layered kinda how a big cake is, you know?"

"Uh, yeah man. Totally."

I bite back a laugh, incredibly proud of my son and so damn amused at the same time. Jordie just opened Pandora's box, and now he's gotta live with the consequences.

"And, and . . ." Bishop pulls in a breath. "I use less water by taking showers because when I was little I took baths, but then I learned that the baths were, um, baths were wasteful, so Mom and Dad let me take showers now and . . ."

Bishop rambles on to his captive audience. Poor

Jordie shoots me a look that pretty much screams *help me*, but I just shrug in response. There's no stopping my kid when he's on a roll.

"Over/under?" Justin asks, nudging me with his elbow.

"What are we betting?"

"How long before Jordie makes his escape."

"Oh, easy. Under ten minutes."

"All right, I'll bet over. Hundred bucks?"

"You're on."

Grant shakes his head in amused disapproval. "You guys are ridiculous."

We all laugh, and even Jordie has to compose himself so as not to offend my kid by giving him anything but his undivided attention. Bishop rattles off fact after fact for so long that Colson starts fussing in my arms, always grumpy when he first wakes up after a deep sleep.

Ruffling his big brother's hair on my way to the door, I carry Colson out into the crisp fall air, rocking him gently against my chest. He wraps one tiny hand around my thumb and hangs on tight.

"Don't worry, bud. Daddy's got you."

BONUS!

In the spirit of bonus material, I bring to you a short story I wrote featuring the new member of the team, Preston. I hope you enjoy it!

GAME FOR LOVE

CHAPTER ONE

Preston

Movement in my bedroom doorway catches my attention.

I was just dozing off, not asleep but not totally awake either, when someone crosses the threshold. It's Essie, I realize.

I really should lock my bedroom door at night. But then I wouldn't have the privilege of these late-night visits, now would I?

Thankfully, it's my roommate, and not say, a hungry bear. Because that would suck. Though I doubt there's any wild bears in the city of Seattle. At least, I hope there's not.

I gaze up at Essie as she pauses beside my bed long enough to slip off her shoes.

"Hey," she murmurs, shrugging out of her thick down coat. "Did I wake you?"

I shake my head.

She went out with friends about the time I announced I was heading to bed. I'm sure it's late now, maybe sometime after two, if I had to guess. I need the sleep because I practiced really hard today.

But with Essie in my bedroom? You do the math.

I'm not getting to sleep anytime soon. I'll probably suffer at practice tomorrow, but it's a price I'm willing to pay.

I lift up on one elbow to gaze at her. Her long wavy hair falls over one shoulder, covering half of her face. Which is too bad, because her face is absolutely stunning. Big blue eyes, high cheekbones, a soft, plush mouth. Her mouth inspires a lot of very wicked thoughts.

"You drunk?" I murmur, my voice coming out deep.

She curses. "No."

"You sure?"

Predictably, an exasperated noise is the only answer I receive. I should know better than to question Essie by now. She keeps me on my toes, that's for sure.

Like her showing up here tonight? Total surprise.

I've asked her out six times this past year. Every time, she's turned me down. It's like my being a professional hockey player doesn't even faze her. I may be an unproven rookie, but still, most girls would be all over that shit. She said it's a personal principle of hers to never date a roommate. Which, believe me, I get.

Fucking them, however? Apparently, that doesn't violate her personal code of ethics. I'm a smart enough man not to point out this inconsistency to her, though. Because . . . aforementioned fucking.

"I'm freezing. Move over," she whispers.

I roll my eyes and make room for her on the bed. She sounds sober enough, but still, this isn't the first time she's shown up in my room after a night of drinking.

In the moonlight filtering through my bedroom window, her blue eyes are unreadable, just like always. Patiently, I wait for her to tell me why she's here. And she does, just not with words. Her firm lips press to mine, and she kisses me.

"Essie?"

"Shut up," she whispers, pressing her mouth to mine again.

Okay, so we're doing this. I'm not one to complain, for the record.

I move her hair from off her face and kiss her back, losing myself to the sensation of her warm mouth, of the heavy weight of her soft tits pressed against my chest. It feels nice, but I'm not stupid enough to pretend this means something to her.

Still, we kiss for several minutes—the soft push and pull of her mouth, the taste of her tongue arousing me. So good.

I pull back just long enough to see her expression. "Did something happen tonight?" I have no idea what could have driven her into my bed, and into my arms.

She doesn't respond, not that I expected her to. This is our secret, and in the light of day, no one would be the wiser, because Essex and I will barely exchange a handful of words come daylight. That's just the way it is.

I kiss her slowly, taking my time. Savoring each press of her full mouth to mine, as though we have all the time in the world. She responds without any hesitation. Her lips part and I touch my tongue to hers, eliciting a resounding groan from somewhere deep inside her chest. I savor that response. She's not as immune to me as she lets on, and I secretly love that.

Leaning up on my forearms, I look down at her, checking to be sure she's still into this. Making sure we're on the same page is important to me.

Her eyes are hazy with desire and her cheeks are flushed. Her fingers graze over the muscles in my chest, and when she lingers and pinches my nipple, I bite my bottom lip to keep from groaning.

Damn.

When she pushes her hand under the elastic in my boxers, I consider stopping her, but only for a second. Because when her warm palm connects with my thickening shaft, I groan. There's no way in hell I'm stopping her now.

I shouldn't want her. She's made it clear we don't have a future. But, inconveniently for me, she's the only girl who makes my pulse spike and my body ache. Essie has rejected my advances so many times, and I've tried dating, but no one interests me like she does.

Normally, I can't stand girls like Essex Kennedy. Smart-mouthed, too clever for her own good. Cruel. Gorgeous, and she knows it. But when the pussy's this good, apparently I'm willing to make a few concessions. And believe me . . . *good* is an understatement. I've never had better. She's an addiction.

Essie releases me only long enough to work her jeans and panties down her legs. I simply watch her in awed fascination.

"What are you waiting for? Do you want this or not?" Her tone is sharp.

"Yeah. Climb aboard." I shove down my boxers and kick them off.

She moves onto my lap, while at the same time rolling her eyes at my incredibly stupid line. Then she slowly sinks down onto my rigid shaft, and I forget how to breathe. Because, *damn*. She's tight and hot and incredible. Her long hair brushes my chest, and when I gaze up at her, her lips are parted.

She pauses for just a second, inhaling as she adjusts to her body's accommodation of mine. It's been months since we've done this, and while my body is eager for her, she takes her time, lowering herself slowly. I won't rush her. She sets the pace—always.

We stopped using condoms sometime last summer. Stupid? Yeah. Incredibly so. But I told her I was clean and wasn't sleeping with anyone else. She said the same, and *voilà*. Here we are.

Essie moves her hips, lifting her ass and rocking against me. It's maddening, and so fucking good. My entire body is drunk with pleasure. I bite my lip to keep from groaning.

"You like riding me?"

"Shut up, Preston."

I groan. "'Cause you look good doing it."

Her movements are quick, determined, and I wonder if she's already getting close. I've learned a lot about Essie in the darkness of my bedroom. Like, for instance, she's highly orgasmic. Sometimes, if I'm lucky, I can even give her two or three, and she leaves me soaking wet, which turns me on something fierce.

"Oh *fuck*. Pres—"

"You were saying?" I grin at her. My voice is

husky, almost desperate.

She comes, shuddering and gasping for breath. I hold her while her body trembles through the release. Then I lift her shirt off over her head and drop it beside my bed. I waste no time filling my hands with her perfect breasts.

"Just a side note . . . your tits look really nice."

With a slow roll of her hips, Essie ignores me, focused solely on her pleasure now.

Which is fine. Because when there's a beautiful woman riding you, you learn to shut the fuck up and let it happen. She works me in hot thrusts, her body gripping mine so tight, I can't help the desperate pleas that fall from my lips.

"That's it. Like that," I say, encouraging her in a rough growl. I pinch her nipples and can't help jacking my hips up in quick succession.

She's quiet as she comes, but she isn't as immune to me as she likes to pretend. Her muscles clench around me and her body shivers. A single sharp inhale is the only clue that she's coming again.

"Yeah, cupcake? Two tonight. You feeling greedy, or you just love my cock that much?"

"I don't love your anything, Preston. Get a clue. I was just horny and didn't want to go home with a rando."

My ego deflates.

When she's done trembling, I grip her trim waist and thrust my hips up off the bed. Deep and fast. I can't hold back anymore, not when my release is right there. My movements become jerky as I pound faster. My balls tighten and I explode, letting out a deep groan.

Essie waits for me to finish, and then she climbs off, gathering her clothes on the side of the bed.

A knot forms in my throat. I hate this part. Not that I'm a cuddler or anything. It just feels so cheap, so temporary when she darts off right afterward.

I reach one hand toward her. "Stay."

She meets my eyes, her expression unreadable. Just like always.

"Please."

With a rare soft look in her eyes, she agrees, climbing back in beside me. "Okay, but only because it's freezing."

I grin. As if the walk back to her bedroom is

so far.

"I know," I whisper. "You're still cold?" I kiss her bare shoulder as she scoots in beside me.

"Not now."

I gather her close and hold her, and surprisingly, she lets me.

My lips linger on the back of her neck, and my chest aches at how good it feels to lie here with her like this. No expectations. No agenda. Just us. For now, anyway. Until she darts off again. I hope that doesn't happen tonight.

"I need to add a few more logs to the stove. Stay put, okay?"

"Mm-hmm." She makes a sleepy sound.

I rise from the bed, tugging on a pair of joggers before I make my way across the frigid wood floors to the wood-burning stove. I've rented a place in the outskirts of town. I wanted a yard for grilling and bonfires in the summer, and I love being out here—there's huge pine trees and plenty of stars at night.

I add three logs to the woodstove and shut the door quickly. Then I climb back in beside Essie and tug her close.

"Sleep, beautiful girl," I say, my mouth near hers.

"You have the worst lines, Preston." She sighs but brings one slender arm around my waist, holding on to me.

I know she feels a lot more for me than she'll ever let on. It's maddening. *Insane*. But I also know that eventually . . . someday . . . I'll get the girl, and she'll love me just as deeply as I love her.

Someday.

Until then, I can be a patient man. While hockey players aren't necessarily known for their patience, for a girl like Essie, I'll wait as long as it takes.

Her breathing evens out and she shifts closer, nestling herself against my chest.

The fact that she's staying tonight, sleeping in my arms? It tells me everything I need to know. A grin takes over my lips as I close my eyes and relax into a peaceful slumber.

She's mine. She just doesn't know it yet.

CHAPTER TWO

Preston

In the morning, I'm actually stunned to see that Essie is still in my bed. A lazy smile drifts over my face when I open my eyes. She's not cuddling with me anymore—she's moved over to the other side of the bed, but she didn't leave. It's gotta count for something, right?

We fell asleep spooning and I held her in my arms, tucked in close to my body. She'd felt so good pressed up against me. I'd drifted off into a restful sleep. And I wake up feeling better than I have in a long time. Go figure.

I adjust my morning wood and watch as Essie blinks open one eye, then the other.

"Hey," she says, voice sleepy.

"Hey," I return, my own voice coming out deep and rough.

"Sorry." She sits up, and rubs one hand over her hair. It's an absolute mess and I kind of love her like this. Sleepy and soft. But I'm sure the claws will come out soon enough. "I didn't mean to sleep in here all night."

"It's all good. I'm glad you did." I stretch and rise from the bed. I'm wearing only boxer briefs which I'd tugged back on last night before falling asleep. Essie's still naked and now my cock is threatening to harden for a very different reason than the aforementioned morning wood.

I do the gentlemanly thing and grab one of my t-shirts for her. It's a Seattle Ice Hawks tee and she accepts it gratefully, tugging it on over her head.

I leave today for four nights to go play two games on the east coast. One in New Jersey and another in Pennsylvania. Essie and I have never had the type of close friendship where we text or call each other, so I probably won't speak to her until I'm back. Which, basically sucks. She's a really cool girl and every new layer I discover about her only makes me want to know more. She's also a really good roommate. I wasn't sure at first about having a chick as a roommate, but she's neat and tidy and quiet. She always cleans the kitchen after she makes food and she doesn't leave makeup or clothes out either. She also makes her bed every-day—I see it when I pass by her room in the hall-way—which is more than I can say for myself. I think the only time I made my bed was that one time my mom came to visit last year. I do wash my sheets weekly, I just never saw the point in making one's bed only to mess it up again every night.

Which means when she walks out of my room in a few minutes, this is it. This is all I will get. Except… an idea occurs to me.

"Hey. If you're not busy…want to grab coffee this morning? Maybe breakfast? That new café is open. We could walk there."

She meets my eyes as though she's considering this, but I can't read her expression.

I'm suddenly nervous like I've never asked a girl out before. My heart thuds in my chest and I just stand there in the center of my room in my un-derwear with a half-hard dick. *Good times.*

"Sure," she says.

Gotta admit I'm a little surprised she said yes. "Cool. Need to shower first, or…?"

Essie shakes her head. "No, I'll just get dressed. Fifteen minutes?"

I nod and watch as she gathers her clothes from my bedroom floor and departs.

In fifteen minutes I can actually accomplish a lot. So I jump in the shower, rub soap all over my body and towel off. I consider shaving, but decide against it. The stubble on my face is good for a few more days at least. Then I brush my teeth and get dressed. I'm actually done in thirteen minutes and then I wait for Essie in the living room.

There's a few texts on my phone from the guys on my team. We have a constant stream of smack-talk in a long chain. It's comprised of memes and bad jokes mostly. I scroll and shake my head, laughing at something Owen has posted. The dude's hilarious.

A minute later, she emerges. She's dressed in jeans and a loose-fitting fuzzy gray sweater that falls off of one shoulder. She's wearing a baseball cap pulled down low and her hair is braided to one side. I try not to notice how effortlessly stunning she is—and fail miserably.

"Ready?" she asks, walking around me toward the door.

She doesn't even give me a once-over. At six foot two, and in incredible shape—it's not the reaction most women give me. It's a little sobering, to be honest. Good thing my ego is robust enough to withstand a few hits.

I shrug and follow her lead. "Yup."

Pocketing my cell phone, I lock the door behind us and Essie and I fall into step together along the sidewalk.

This part of town isn't super walkable, but there's an organic grocery store on the corner and then a strip mall with a dentist's office. In the same building, a new café opened this summer. There's outdoor seating, but it's too cold for that this time of year. In fact, Essie huddles close to me as we walk. I don't hate it.

"Have you ever watched one of my games?"

She told me when we first met that she wasn't a hockey fan. At the time, I figured maybe that was for the best. I couldn't imagine living with some fangirl who was going to bug me for my teammate's autographs or free tickets all the time. But now, I'm curious. Is she interested in what I do at all? Does she care? Is she impressed? Doesn't seem like it.

She shakes her head, looking down at our shoes as we walk. "No, sorry. Can't say I have."

"How's school?" I ask, needing a topic change.

Essie meets my gaze. I can't help but remember back to last night when she was perched above me like a goddess, practically fucking the life out of me. I remember how flushed her skin was, those hot little whimpering sounds she made when she tipped over the edge—not once, but twice. I need to know what makes her tick—what makes her push me away during the daylight hours, but seek out comfort and affection in my bed at night.

"It's …" She releases a big, heavy sigh.

"That good, huh?" I push open the door for the café and the chalkboard sign directs us to seat ourselves.

Essie leads the way, choosing a booth by the windows. I slide in across from her.

She orders a large coffee and a pumpkin muffin. I order a bagel and a small coffee.

"I'm taking eighteen credit hours this semester so I can be done next spring, and it's … *a lot*." She emphasizes the word with a nervous laugh.

"If anyone can handle it, it's you. I've seen how

hard you work."

She gives me an appreciative smile. I know she's nervous about graduating next year and finding a job. She mentioned something about paying off her student loans once.

Admittedly, I don't know a ton about Essex Kennedy. She's a somewhat guarded girl.

I know she grew up two hours east of here. I know she needs coffee before she can function in the morning. I know she's a night owl, often listening to soft music in her room late into the evening. I know that she writes in a journal, and takes her phone calls on the back porch for privacy. I know that one time, after one of those phone calls, she was crying when she came inside and I gathered her up in my arms and held her while she sobbed, comforting her by rubbing her back and letting her soak my t-shirt with tears. We never spoke about that day again. I know she loves pizza—all varieties, and that she would love to adopt a cat someday. And I know that I want her to be mine.

She's not too demanding. She's not too talkative, but she's not too quiet either.

Basically, Essie is the Goldilocks of hookups.

Technically I have it made. I should just leave

well enough alone. But of course I can't do that.

She tells me more about her econ class while I finish off my bagel. I could listen to her talk about this for hours. Unfortunately, I have a plane to catch. I check the time on my phone discreetly. Well, not that discreetly, because Essie pauses and gives me a pointed look. "Do you need to go?"

I grin and nod at her sheepishly. "The plane leaves in two hours. I need to go home and put on a suit. Grab my bags." Drive to the airfield.

"I never understood the whole suit thing. Weird rule if you ask me."

I nod in agreement and motion to our server to bring us our check.

Fishing my wallet from my pocket, I place my black card down on top of the check.

"I can pay for myself," she says, grabbing her wallet.

This is the first and only time Essie's been out to eat with me. It's not a date, but we did sleep together last night. I know I should be more sensitive about these things and not so boxed-in with my masculine-thinking on this, but my manners just won't let me. "I've got it."

"Not happening." She levels me with a look and I fight off a smile.

"Split it?" I suggest.

The bill is like twelve dollars, asking her to pay for half would be ridiculous, but here we are.

Geez this girl is a tough nut to crack. She won't even let me spring for a coffee the morning after.

A few minutes later, we start back on our walk back home. Neither of us talks about last night but I wonder if she's still thinking about it like I am. I'll be thinking about it for a while, I'm sure, probably while I fist my cock under the sheets tonight in New Jersey…

"One of these days, Essie. I'm gonna figure you out…"

She laughs, and I love the sound of it. It's light and somehow husky at the same time. "Don't count on it."

She's probably right. I chuckle and shake my head.

When we reach the house, there's a random dude standing on my porch. He looks like a hipster type with artfully torn jeans and red Converse tennis shoes.

Essie pauses, looking uncertain.

"You know him?"

She nods, giving me a sheepish look. "From school, yeah."

When we approach, he turns in our direction. I have a good six inches on the dude and at least thirty pounds—which is my way of saying, I could take him if I needed to.

I've never been the possessive, territorial type, but with Essie? I guess she brings out a different side of me. And the more time we spend together, the more of her time and attention I want. I don't like the idea of a guy showing up here to see her. Especially when I'm about to leave for most of the week.

"Oh, hey Warren."

I clear my throat and unlock the door while they exchange small talk. Apparently he has a question on a paper that's due this week.

While I gather my stuff for the week, I overhear Warren ask her out to a poetry reading on campus next Friday night. My stomach tightens.

"We could grab dinner beforehand," he says.

I don't want to hear her response so I close my bedroom a little more loudly than I intend to. *Whoops.* I'm being an asshole, but what did anyone expect? This girl was in my arms not even twelve hours ago while I pressed sucking kisses into her skin. While I emptied myself into her eager body. Now there's a dude sniffing up her skirt in my own damn living room?

Once I'm ready, I gather up my bags and head down the hall.

"Well, you two have fun. I'll see you, okay?" I say, turning to Essie. I'm trying to keep my anger and frustration in check. It was my bed she woke up in this morning, and now I have to leave her here with some dude with an eyebrow ring while I go off for four days and four nights.

"Preston…" she calls when I'm halfway out the door.

"Yeah?" I turn to face her.

Her blue eyes meet mine and she toys with the end of her braid. "Is your game tonight or tomorrow?"

My stomach does a weird flip. "Tomorrow. Why?"

She licks her lips and gives me a kind look. "Because. I might just watch it."

Warren rolls his eyes. I resist the urge to flip him the middle finger. But then I gaze back at Essie and my mouth lifts in a lazy smile. "Cool. See you on Tuesday."

I've never looked forward to a Tuesday so much in my entire life.

CHAPTER THREE

Essex

I make it a point to not be at home on Tuesday. I feel like a bitch, but this right here is why I never should have gotten involved with Preston in the first place. Sex makes things weird. And hiding out from my own home in favor of spending the day in the campus library is exhibit A on the *where did I go wrong* scale.

Part of me doesn't want to see his hurt expression when I tell him I didn't end up watching his game after all. Part of me wants to forget the disappointment in his eyes when he saw Warren waiting for me on the porch.

I know Preston wants us to be more, but I just can't commit to that. He's great as a roommate, and I'll be honest, he's absolutely incredible as a hookup partner, but we'll never be more.

And okay, I'll admit, his dick is impressive. As are his skills in the bedroom. Somehow I always manage to cross the finish line at least twice, if not three times when I'm with him—something that has never happened to me with anyone else. Ever.

Not that there's been anyone else in a long time. Working full-time and going to school full-time simultaneously eats up all my free time. That, and generally worrying about my future takes up a surprising amount of energy.

Preston's a sweet guy—as uncomplicated as white bread. And my life is anything but simple. My dad's in prison—it's not something I've ever admitted out loud. And I work my ass off to help both him make restitution, and to save for my future. I have big goals and I'm going to make something of myself. I don't have time for a man. Plus, we have nothing in common aside from the fact that we both like orgasms.

My last relationship went south in the most disastrous way, and I'm still not over the betrayal. So forgive me if I'm not ready to jump into anything resembling a commitment with a man.

I dated Kyle for three years, we grew up together and to be quite honest, I always thought we would get married someday. We moved in together and everything was perfect. Until it wasn't.

My younger sister decided to take a gap year in between high school and college and needed a place to stay for a little while—I talked Kyle into letting her move in with us. Which honestly wasn't that hard. He and my sister, Camyrn, were always close. She was a few years younger than us, but they shared a similar sense of humor and even had inside jokes between the two of them. And Camyrn was going through a rough patch—trying to figure out what she wanted to do with her life. Which, is you know, a daunting task when you're nineteen years old. I was happy to help.

Kyle made sure she was included and even brought her home little gifts—candy just because, or once a little plastic trophy that said, *Congratulations! You made it through the week.*

I worked a lot and between that and school, I felt bad leaving her alone at the apartment so much, so I was grateful to Kyle for keeping her company. But then they grew closer—almost oddly so. I started to suspect something might be going on between them—but pushed the idea away, sure I was only being insecure.

After Camryn left her phone on the counter and I saw a text from Kyle that I was never meant to see—I discovered they were sleeping together. When I confronted Kyle, he denied it, but when I pressed my sister, she finally told me the truth.

They'd been having an emotional affair for months, and a physical relationship for almost just as long. Apparently Camryn pushed him to break things off with me so they could be together, and when he wouldn't—he was too spineless—she intentionally got pregnant.

So yeah my life is basically a Jerry Springer show.

Camryn is due any day now and I haven't spoken to either of them in months. They live together in the apartment he and I once shared. My name is still on the lease, but I just needed out of there. When I saw the listing for this room in Preston's house in the suburbs—far away from them, I jumped at the chance.

Now it's all I can do to keep myself busy enough that I don't have time to think about Kyle or my sister or my soon-to-be- niece or nephew that I wish I was more excited about.

I decided months ago that Kyle wouldn't get

anymore of my brain space, but that eventually I would have to make up with my sister. Because, family, and all that. In my opinion, though, us making up would only start once she said the words, "I'm sorry," which had yet to leave her lips.

Which is why the first time I hooked up with Preston had been completely unexpected.

We'd gone out drinking with a group of friends and when we got back home it was late—almost one in the morning. I should have gone to bed. Instead I agreed to watch a superhero film with him since we'd spent much of the night debating which franchise was better—Marvel or Star Wars. We'd sat down on the couch and then Preston turned to me. My mind drifts back to that night and my skin grows warm all over…

My roommate's lips are on my neck. My brain sputters and freezes. I should stop him, but I don't. Because it feels really, really good. His mouth is apparently very talented and I haven't been kissed in a very long time. I'm sure in the morning I'm going to regret this, but I push my fingers into his hair and tug, directing his mouth up to mine. I would never have imagined that a big, bulky hockey player could kiss so well, but he does. Holy hell. Preston's tongue makes a slow circle around mine and my panties start to get wet. The man is a damn good kisser. I feel dizzy and a little weak. I know if he takes me to his bed, I won't be able to resist. Even if it is a mistake.

I'm a business student and he's a jock. We should have nothing in common, but don't tell that to my body because wow my libido roars to life, very happy with my current decision of letting Preston suck on my tongue.

With a suddenly increased pulse, I shake my head, clearing away the thoughts.

I suck at picking men. Don't even get me started on Kyle again. And then there's my dad is doing time for tax fraud and I'm trying to make something of myself and my life which doesn't include going all fan-girl over some hockey player.

Yes, Preston is attractive, but he wouldn't understand my life. His mom sends him a package with chocolate chip cookies at least once a month and presents on his birthday. I only know this because he turned twenty-four last month and there was balloons and streamers and gifts, and all kinds of shit here. It took up half the dining room.

I can't hook up with him anymore, I know that deep down. Does it suck? Yeah kinda, but so does being an adult. Welcome to my life.

CHAPTER FOUR

Preston

I don't see Essie until Wednesday after practice. She returns home from class and drops her laptop bag at the front door.

"Hey," I say, lifting my eyes from my phone. I've been watching North Carolina's power plays and trying to get a handle on what our penalty-kill strategy should be going into Saturday's game.

"Hey." She sounds tired. She looks it too.

"You've been busy, huh?"

She nods, and tucks a length of dark hair behind one ear. "Yeah. I got home late last night. Hopefully I didn't wake you when I came in."

"You didn't." A lopsided smile lifts one side of my mouth. "Not that I would have minded."

"Perv," she mutters, rolling her eyes.

"Did you catch the game?" I ask, watching her move into the kitchen to grab a bottle of water from the fridge.

"No." She takes a long drink. "I had to write a paper on IPOs."

I nod, and try not to feel disappointed. "That's cool. IPOs are very important."

She laughs. "Do you even know what an IPO is?"

I lift one brow. "Of course."

She doesn't look convinced.

"Want to hang out? Watch a movie?" I pat the spot on the couch next to me.

Essie lets out a long sigh and rubs her temples. Then she replaces the cap on her water bottle and turns to face me. Even before the next words leave her mouth, I know I'm not going to like them. "Look, Preston, you're a great guy. And I really like living here."

"Okay…" My voice comes out in a croak.

"And the hookups were…" She stops herself, holding up one hand. "Were, *you know*, fun."

Fun?

That wasn't just sex. I don't care what she says. That was two people worshipping each other, connecting on a level deeper than I have with anyone—ever. How does she not see this? We're perfect together. In the bedroom, anyways. And I have a feeling we would be perfect outside of it too if she'd only give us a shot. But Essie is determined to keep me at a distance.

"But I don't do feelings," she continues, meeting my eyes. "And I'm not looking for the whole boyfriend thing. It's just not my scene."

"Okay, that's fine," I hear myself say but the words sound hollow. I hate this. Hate that I'm not enough for her, but I keep my expression neutral. I act like the aloof hockey playboy everyone probably expects me to be anyways and give her a weak smile.

Essie nods once and then grabs her water and her bag and retreats to her bedroom, silently closing the door behind her—sending a message that's as clear as day—she wants to be alone.

Essie isn't just somewhere to park my dick when I'm bored. She means a lot to me. Not that I can tell her that. It would probably send her running for the hills. She's perfect. Beautiful. Smart. Sexy as fuck. Deciding I need to blow off some steam, I grab my keys and head to the gym.

I try lifting weights, but I'm too distracted.

I get on the treadmill to run and only make it a mile. God, this sucks. I haven't been this spun-up over a girl since my high school crush dumped me right before prom. I'd felt like a loser back then, unlovable. I feel the exact same way now to be honest. Apparently I'm not one of those guys who can do casual hookups…although it never seemed to be a problem before Essie.

I decide to text my teammate Jordie's wife Harper. She's really cool, and very no-holds-barred. She's a couple of years older than me and I've found myself gravitating to her for advice. I shoot off a text to both her and Jordie since I don't want my buddy to think it's weird that I text his wife.

Help meeee, my text says.

Jordie is the first to reply. What'd you do now, you big idiot?

There's no sense in beating around the bush.

I trust Jordie and Harper completely with my secrets. Fell for the wrong girl?

Jordie replies again. This is Harper's domain. Babe?

I wait to see if she'll reply, but she's probably at work. I frown and stare down at my phone, like I can somehow will her to write back.

Harp—I need relationship advice. I add a begging hands emoji for good measure.

Come over tonight, Harper finally replies. I'm making spaghetti and can dole out some advice.

Perfect. I'll bring red wine. Love you guys. I stuff my phone in my pocket and decide to push all thoughts of Essie out of my brain until at least tonight.

Over bowls of spaghetti Bolognese, I spill my story to Jordie and Harper. She looks at me with a concerned expression and urges me on. Jordie, on the other hand, barely takes a breath as he shovels forkfuls of pasta into his mouth. *Classic.*

I tell them everything—the hot hookups we've

shared, the fact that she let me hold her all night as we slept this last time, I even tell them about Warren and how I felt like beating him with a hockey stick.

"I'm totally pathetic, right?" I say once I've finished.

Harper gazes at me from across their dining table, swirling the ruby colored liquid in her wine glass. "Not necessarily."

"Go on," I urge.

"Here's what you need to do." There's an evil glint in her eye and I lean forward in rapt interest as Harper tells me all the things.

Oh, this is gonna be good…

CHAPTER FIVE

Preston

At my friend Harper's urging, I agreed to be set up on a blind date.

Idiotic, I know.

But Harper was convinced that if Essie thought I was moving on with someone else, it would force her to reveal her true feelings on the subject. The subject of how she feels about me.

Since I'm an idiot and was also desperate, I agreed.

Harper thought me going out with someone else would make Essie jealous, or make her realize that she does want to be with me. It was a longshot.

The only person they could come up with on short notice was Harper's hair stylist, Veronica.

Veronica has purple hair and a lot of tattoos. We got Thai food and then I dropped her off at home. As far as I'm concerned, it was a colossal waste of time because yesterday when I told Essie I had a date tonight, she'd smiled at me and said, "Cool. Have fun." Like it was the least interesting piece of information she'd ever heard.

Fuck my life, am I right?

I spent most of the date talking about Essie, which was probably not very cool of me. But Veronica was kind about it.

I make it home by nine—which should tell you how not-great my date went. But Essie's not here, so I sulk to my bedroom in defeat.

I'm lying on my bed texting with Harper and Jordie when there's a light knock on my door.

My heart rate kicks up.

"Yeah?" I call and drop the phone onto my bed.

The door opens, and Essie peeks inside. "Are you awake?"

"Yeah."

"You up for company?"

"Sure." My pulse starts to pound in anticipation. I move over and Essie sits down beside me on the bed.

She yawns and I pat the pillow. "Lay down. You tired?"

She nods sheepishly and lays down on my pillow, curling onto her side to look up at me.

Man, she's pretty. Her hair across my pillow is a welcome sight but I try not to be creepy by staring. She looks tired tonight. Between her internship and her classes, I'm sure she is. I wish I could do something to help her, but I'm not sure what. Essie is also very independent and I wouldn't want to make her feel helpless. Something tells me she's not good at accepting help anyway.

My phone lights up with another text from Harper or Jordie, but I ignore it.

"How was your date?" she asks.

I lay down beside her and gaze up at the ceiling. There's a crack in the plaster in the shape of a sealion. I debate with myself about how honest to be with her. If the point, according to Harper is to make her jealous…I should lead her to believe it went well, right? On the other hand, I won't lie to Essie.

I swallow. "It was okay. Her name was Veronica. My teammate's wife introduced us."

She gives me an uneven look. "And was she *wife* material?"

I bark out a laugh. "Uh. Next question."

Essie doesn't pepper me with questions though. If there's one thing we know how to do, it's how to share a comfortable silence.

Essie closes her eyes and lets out a long slow breath. She's relaxed around me and completely comfortable. Something about that is…actually kind of annoying. I poke her in the ribs. Her eyes open.

"You've got to give me a real shot before you decide this won't work."

Her eyes stay on mine.

"One date. I get to wine and dine you." *And sixty-nine you*, I mentally add because I have the maturity of a sixteen-year-old. Thankfully I don't say that part out loud.

One of her eyebrows lifts. "Okay."

"Okay."

CHAPTER SIX

Preston

Part of me still can't believe that Essie agreed to this date. I've asked her out no less than a dozen times over the past nine months that she's lived here. I'd gotten used to getting shot down. Which means the fact that she finally said yes has thrown me off my game.

I spend a ridiculous amount of time planning our date, researching where to go, reading restaurant reviews and mapping out our way around the city just so there were no surprises. The last thing I wanted to do was get stuck in a construction zone or waste our time in needless traffic. Then I spend almost just as long showering, manscaping and getting ready. I want tonight to be perfect—to show Essie that we can be so much more than just fuckbuddies.

Just when I'm about ready, there's a sudden knock on my bedroom door.

"I need to talk to you," Essie's voice floats through the door. I open it and she steps inside carrying a decently sized flesh colored sex toy. I might have been a little jealous if not for my own more than adequately sized dick.

"Um Ess?" I clear my throat. "I thought we'd go to dinner first. I made us reservations at—"

She holds up one hand. "Stop talking."

A sudden wave of panic flashes through me. Is the toy for her, or am I its intended target? *What is happening?* I must say this part out loud because Essie sits down on the side of my bed. She's still holding the toy. It's wrapped tightly in one fist. "This was supposed to be the only penis in my life." She waves the toy at me.

"Um okay…" My brain short-circuits, but I'm trying really hard to roll with the punches here.

"And then you came along, so sweet and kind and patient. God you've been so patient." She meets my eyes and there's a pained expression on her face.

My stomach sinks. She's about to cancel. I can see it written all over her. Her shoulders are tense and her eyes have a firm look about them.

"I'll I've done is push you away. I know I'm a mess okay?"

"You're not a mess. You're focused. I get that. Hell, I respect it a ton."

"Well, thank you, I think. But it's time we had a talk."

She pats the spot on the bed next to her and I take a seat.

"All right."

I'm guessing this is where she lets me down easy. Where she sits me down and tells me once and for all that things are over between us. Not that they had ever really begun, a couple of hot hook-ups aside. It was all over before it even started. The look of defeat on her face says it all.

"What do you want to talk about?" My voice sounds wooden and hollow, but I'm not exactly feeling thrilled right now.

"This." She motions between us. "I just can't,

Preston. I'm sorry. You're an incredibly sweet guy, but my life…" She swallows.

"Tell me." I lean in closer. "Tell me whatever it is you need to say. Tell me why we wouldn't work."

Her schedule is busy, sure, but so is mine. I'll take what I can get and I'll never pressure her. I know how important school is.

Essie clears her throat. And then she begins. It's with an incredible sense of calm that she relays to me the facts of her life. There are no tears as she tells me that her mother left when she was three years old, and her sister was just a newborn. No hiccupping sobs when she explains that her father, who had raised her, had never been one for hugs or I love yous. No halting breaths when she tells me that he went to prison two years ago for tax fraud. Apparently, he'd been into some shady business practices.

And I play the part well too, I don't gasp or recoil in alarm. I just sit beside her, listening to everything and rubbing the back of her hand with my knuckles.

She saves the bombshell for the end—the real reason she's gun-shy when it comes to relationships. Her ex-fiancé had started sleeping with her sister. Camyrn is pregnant and due any day, and Essie said for her own sanity, she'd had to cut both of them out of her life for a while. I don't judge her for this at all.

"Fuck. I'm sorry. That's a lot," I say when I think she's finally finished.

She glances up at me and meets my eyes. We're both quiet. The toy now sits on the bed beside her. "I guess it is, isn't it?"

I lift one hand to her face and stroke her cheek. "None of that is going to scare me away. I still want a shot with you."

Her gaze drops from mine. "Well, it scares me okay? I promised myself I was going to take a long break from men and that I would not get tangled up with some guy again and it's what… nine months later and I'm ready to cast that vow aside and why? Because the sex is good between us?" I flinch. "I'm sorry, Preston. I just can't. I respect myself more than that. If I can't keep a promise I made to myself," she shakes her head, "I just can't do this, okay?"

And because I don't want to be the cause of any more of her pain, I say, "Okay."

Essie rises from the bed, grabs the toy and

leaves me alone with my thoughts.

I release an agonizingly slow breath. My first thought is, about how I want to get really hammered on tequila shots. Then I realize the whole night I'd meticulously planned is ruined.

The girl I'd been so desperate to get to know—to peel back the layers on—has a lot more hard edges than I realized.

Essie has lived a hard life. She's young, but she's already endured more than most people twice her age.

I couldn't get over how exceptionally calm and composed she remained throughout our talk. She had the strength of ten women and quite honestly, all that little talk did was make me fall for her even more.

Forget the tequila. All I want is for Essie to see herself the way I see her.

CHAPTER SEVEN

Back inside my bedroom, I close the door and let out a huge sigh. I never let people in—never spill the dirty secrets of my life—ever. And believe me, I've come close a few times. There have been friends in college I've gotten close to, but ultimately decided it wasn't worth it. But telling Preston about my dad and sister and Kyle and the baby… all I feel is relief. Someone finally knows the truth. If he hates me now or looks down on me, that's on him. I've spoken my truth. I tuck my fleshy-friend who I've lovingly nicknamed Bob back inside my nightstand drawer.

Since my evening plans are now ruined, I slip off my shoes and grab my laptop bag before settling on my bed. I might as well get some studying done. I have three chapters to read for my comparative mythology class—which I took because I thought it'd be a fun elective—boy, was I wrong. And I also have a paper due in my economics class next week that I haven't even started yet. I pull my materials from my bag just as there's a knock on my door.

I figured Preston would leave me alone the rest of the night—probably even give me a wide berth tomorrow too. But it's been what, four minutes and he's already knocking on my door. Am I really ready to face him? But what's my alternative—climb out the bedroom window?

My pulse quickens. "Come in," I call.

Preston opens the door, but doesn't enter. He just stands in the doorway gazing at me with a dark expression.

• • •

Preston

I couldn't just leave this thing alone between us—which is why minutes after Essie shut me out, I'm knocking on her door.

"Come in," she calls.

I open it and my lungs stop working. She's beautiful. Sitting on her bed with a pen in her mouth and textbooks spread out all over in front of her.

I do what any desperate man would do—I start blurting things out.

"I know you think your life is too complicated, but it's not. Not for me."

She blinks at me and then gestures me forward into her bedroom.

I cross the threshold and sit beside her on the bed. "If you don't want this, and you're sure that you'd be better off alone—tell me to leave and I promise I will. I'll never bother you again. You can keep living here and we'll be roommates, and that's it."

My heart is hammering because I'm pretty sure that's exactly what she's about to tell me.

"But if even a small part of you is into me…"

She gives me a kind look. "You know I am, Preston."

"Then let me be there for you."

Her eyes latch onto mine and she gives me a small nod. "I'm scared."

"Don't be," I say, gathering her up in my arms. "Your ex is the worst and your sister made a huge mistake by getting with him, but that's on them. And your dad…well, it sounds like he's paying for his mistakes too. But you don't need to suffer because they messed up. You get to live for *you*, okay? Do things that make you happy. Put yourself first."

She nestles herself in closer, pressing her face into the stubble on my neck. "Thanks, Preston."

"For what?" I hold her close, and man it feels good.

"For not judging me. And for, well, everything. You've been so good to me while I tried again and again to push you away."

"I get why you did it."

She lifts her face and I lower mine, and then our lips are pressing together. It's not what I expected, but kissing Essie is a magical experience, so I'm not about to complain.

"We could still go to dinner," I say when we part a few minutes later.

She lifts her eyes to mine and smiles. "Okay."

The evening that I thought was ruined turns out to be anything but. We make it in time for our reservations at the new Italian place. It's every bit as romantic as the reviews made it seem. We share glasses of red wine, and tiramisu—plus we manage to eat impressive amounts of pasta. Then we take a walk around the city, stopping to listen to a jazz musician on the corner. Essie leans her head on my shoulder and we sway together under the moonlight.

Things are going better than expected. I tell her about the late night showing of *The Notebook* at the historic cinema, but she shakes her head. "Let's go home."

They're the three best words I've ever heard.

I keep myself distracted during the drive home by peppering Essie with questions.

"Chocolate or vanilla?"

"Both!" she shouts enthusiastically.

"Horror movies or comedy?"

"Both? Sorry," she laughs. "I really suck at this game."

I chuckle along with her. "No, it's okay. Variety is the spice of life."

By the time we make it home, the temperature has dropped and there's a light rain falling outside. Inside, we shrug out of our jackets and I can't help it, I lift Essie into my arms. She wraps her legs around my hips and I kick off my boots before I begin carrying her back to my bedroom.

I place her on the center of the bed. Man she looks good there.

She kisses me and my body responds immediately. When she notices, she brings one hand to the front of my jeans and strokes my hardening erection.

Things are moving really fast, and while I normally wouldn't complain about this—I want Essie to know she means more to me than some sprint-to-the-finish-line encounter.

The desire to empty the contents of my balls makes it difficult to form coherent thoughts, but I do my best.

"Wait." I sound breathless, like I just skated a four-minute shift. "We should slow down. We should talk. Maybe have a drink."

"Okay." She tips her chin, considering this. "I'll have a drink."

"Do you like Japanese whisky?"

"Sure?"

I chuckle at her uncertainty. "Stay right there."

I rush to the kitchen for two glasses and pour us each a measure of the whisky I save for special occasions. There's not an occasion more special than this as far as I'm concerned.

Over sips of whisky, we lounge on my bed and talk. I tell her some of my past—like growing up with a single mom, and how hockey became my whole world.

I tell her about how we didn't grow up with much money and that for fun we'd walk to the park with a picnic lunch. Some of my best memories from childhood are sitting in the grass, looking up at the clouds move.

She leans back against my pillows, glass of whisky in her hand. "What was the thing you thought signified that someone was rich back then? Mine was if you had children's flavored toothpaste. If you had the extra four dollars to spring for the bubblegum flavored toothpaste, clearly your family had money. And for sure a pool…if you had a pool, in my mind, you were insanely rich."

"Toothpaste? Really?" I chuckle at her.

She nods. "I know. But my dad only bought regular and everyone used it. One bathroom house."

It sounds like maybe we're more similar than she ever realized. I grew up without much extra and learned early on not to take anything for granted.

"Mine was having a basketball hoop in the driveway. I always wanted one of those. Oh, and maybe having cable TV too. That would have been nice."

She nods. Then she sets her glass down on my nightstand and crawls across the bed toward me. My heart accelerates as I watch her move. And when she plants herself in my lap, I struggle for oxygen.

"You're a good man, Preston."

I touch her face, stroking my thumb along her cheek. "And you're a good girl, Ess."

A slow, crooked smile lifts her mouth. I'm not convinced she believes me. It's something we'll have to work on.

I push my hands under her shirt, loving the feel of her soft skin under my fingertips. When I remove her shirt, Essie lifts her arms. Then she strips herself of her bra, and I suck in a sharp inhale. She's beautiful. We've hooked up before—but never like this. Never face to face with the lights on.

Her hands fumble with my belt and I help her out, freeing it from my pants. Then she draws down my fly and I forget how to breath. My boxers are pushed out of the way as she works her hand under the elastic.

I can't help the involuntary groan that escapes me when she curls her fist around me. Her hand moves over my length in hot, eager strokes and I groan, knees trembling.

"I need to be inside you."

"Yes," she agrees. "Should we use protection… or?"

"What do you mean?" My pulse is going crazy because Essie's still in my lap. And she's still topless.

"I'm asking how well your date went the other night and if…" She lifts one eyebrow at me.

"My date?" *Veronica?* "No. God, no." I shake

my head. She doesn't realize the date was a rouse. She's the only woman I want. "I haven't been with anyone but you." I guess I'll have to fess up to the plot to make her jealous…

"Good." She kisses me again. The friction in my lap is making me insane.

"What about you … Warren?"

"Ew. No."

I chuckle into her kiss. "Good." That is very good news, because I have a hard time picturing her with any man who isn't me.

"If we do this…you're my girlfriend. You know that, right?"

Essie's eyes find mine and I struggle to read her expression.

"Girlfriend?" she repeats the word, a quizzical look in her eyes.

"It's a stupid word, I know. But there's no one else. Try with me?"

"Okay," she agrees and my lips are on hers before she even gets the word out.

I feel like I won the lottery. Finally, a shot with Essie. A real shot. I'm deliriously happy.

But then Essie is bringing one hand between us and lifting on her knees… and all other thoughts fade away. When she joins us, my hips lift from the bed and I get us the rest of the way there—filling her in one smooth stroke.

"Yes. Preston." She groans out my name and clings to my shoulders as I hold her tight and pummel into her body again and again.

It's perfect and I'm lost to the sensation. To the sound her halting breaths leaving her lips, to the way she feels around me—tight and warm and wonderful.

It's only a few minutes later when Essie's first orgasm sneaks up on her. She clings to me, riding out the waves.

"Yes, baby. *Fuck*," I groan.

I keep up my pace—steady, but not overeager and … Essie gasps. Here comes my second reward. I love this. Love how responsive she is.

She gasps again and repeats my name. It's the best sound. I could do this all night. Okay, that's a lie. I'm already dangerously close to the edge.

I'm feeling greedy tonight, and since I suspect she's got one more in her, I don't let up. Not even as my body threatens to betray me, not even as the pleasure becomes so unbearable, I grunt out a long groan.

Finally, I'm rewarded. Essie quivers in my arms and curses under her breath, riding me hard. It's too much and I go off like a rocket, coming so hard I almost pass out.

After, she laughs. I turn and give her a questioning look. "What's so funny?"

She chuckles again, breathless. "I have a confession to make."

I lift one eyebrow. "I'm listening."

"You're the only guy to make me do that, you know?"

"Do *that*?" Oh, the multiple-O thing... *Interesting.*

She nods, shyly.

"See. I knew you were mine."

Essie doesn't argue. She grins at me, and uses her fingers to turn my cheek toward hers, where she plants a sweet kiss. "Seems like it."

A Collection of Deleted and Bonus Scenes from the original
HOT JOCKS SERIES

PLAYING FOR KEEPS

Justin

As I enter the bedroom, two things happen simultaneously. The first is that my eyes are assaulted by the vision of my best friend naked. *Gah!* The second is that my stomach tightens as I take in the scene around him.

He's bent over at the waist and handcuffed to the headboard. Lying on the floor between his parted feet is a purple glittery dildo.

What the actual fuck?

Owen groans in relief when he sees me. "Thank God. Took you long enough. Get me the fuck out of here."

The uneasy feeling inside my chest grows with each step closer I take. "What the fuck happened, dude?"

Owens hesitates for a second, hanging his head.

"Revenge happened."

My eyebrows jump up. "This was a revenge fuck?"

Owen doesn't answer right away, he just hangs his head in shame.

I locate the key to the handcuffs on a nearby dresser and get to work unlocking each of his wrists while trying not to make eye contact with any exposed body parts. I've seen it all before in the locker room, but this just feels different. It feels fucking wrong.

He grunts as finally free him, rubbing at his wrists which each bear a faint red mark.

"I guess that wasn't the first time I picked up that redhead from the bar. And when she realized I didn't remember her, she freaked out. In my defense, it was two years ago, and she'd cut her hair."

"So she just left you like this?" I look up at the ceiling while he locates his boxers and jeans and begins getting dressed.

"It was a little more involved than that," Owen says, his eyes wandering to his purple glittery friend on the floor.

For a second I consider ignoring the elephant in

the room, because part of me really does *not* want to know the particulars of this little sexcapade gone wrong. But then the logical part of my brain points out that this situation Owen's found himself in could provide ammunition for years to come. And knowing I'll be able to hang this over his head anytime I want something? Well, let's just say I'm willing to put my own discomfort aside in favor of knowing the truth.

"So did she...?"

"Yup."

"And the ..." My eyes stray toward the toy left behind.

"You don't want to know," he snaps.

"Oh but I do." I grin wryly.

Owen groans and shakes his head, as if dislodging a painful memory. "Can we please just fucking go?"

I hold up one hand. "Fine. You're right. I probably don't want to know."

"Damn right you don't. And I can't believe you brought my sister."

I shrug. "She was worried. We were all out together when I got your text."

He exhales slowly, grabbing his discarded shirt from the floor. "Let's go."

"Happily. After you," I remark.

Owen stops me at the door to the hallway with a hand pressed into my chest. "And if you tell any of the guys about this, I will fucking end you."

I grin. "How about *thank you, Justin for saving my ass*. Literally," I add.

He rolls his eyes and heads out the door to face Elise.

ALL THE WAY

Angel,

I've never written a love letter before, and so I'm sure this is going to sound cheesy. But the thing is, I really don't give a shit. I love you, and if this note makes you smile—even a little bit, then it's all worth it.

I should also add, I'm not even sure why I'm writing one now. I guess it's because I'm missing you. Or because at the team dinner earlier tonight, the guys started harassing me about what a douchey boyfriend I am. Both are true.

They might have gotten a hold of the knowledge that I occasionally send you dick pics while on the road that say 'he misses you'.

I think I have Justin and Elise to thank for sharing that tidbit of info. But the thing is, I'm not ashamed. I do miss you when I travel. And so does my dick. We agree on most things these days. Kisses from you make us smile. Everything is better when you're near. We live to please you. Sorry. Enough about my dick. I got side-tracked. But hey, it's one of my favorite topics...

What I really wanted to tell you is you're the strongest person I know—which is saying something because I'm constant-ly surrounded by hockey players, which are known for being pretty damn tough. I mean last year Asher skated with pulled groin for two games, and when Grant dislocated his shoulder in the third pe-riod against Montreal, he didn't even flinch—practically fought our coach about sitting out. Although coach made him, because that's just crazy. Whoops. I got distracted again, didn't I? Anyway, like I was saying, you're the toughest person I know. Watching you take back your power and fight for your future was so inspiring. I don't know if I've ever told you that. Getting to be the man by your side when you decided that just because life had handed you a pile of crap, you were not broken. I'm proud of you. And I'm so glad you're mine. Now and forever.

The sound of someone pounding on my hotel room door momentarily interrupts my train of thought and I heft out a sigh as I get to my feet.

When I pull open the door Asher is smirking at me. My six-foot four sandy-haired teammate from Southern California is the very definition of easygoing, but that doesn't mean I want him to know what I'm up to.

"Hey," I say, shielding the door frame with my body.

"Can I come in?" he asks, raising his eyebrows.

With a defeated sigh, I step to the side. "Sure."

Three attempts at writing this love letter are scattered on the bed along with a pen and notebook. I'm hoping he can't make out my horrible handwriting. Although I'd rather be made fun of for my penmanship than what's in this letter. Everything in there is straight from my heart, and I won't apologize for it.

He flops down into the desk chair, ignoring my bed and the love letter it contains completely. Thank goodness.

"You okay?" he asks, eyeing me.

"Why wouldn't I be?" I narrow my eyes.

"Because everyone was giving you shit at dinner."

I shrug. "That's nothing new." The guys liked to harass each other and I'd developed a thick skin over the years. It came with the territory of being on a hockey team.

"It's just because they're jealous, you know."

"I doubt that." I scoff.

Asher glares at me. "Dude. They totally are. Everyone knows you and Becca are the golden couple—completely in love and committed to each other. The younger, single guys talk a big game, but you and I both know they wish they could find someone as loving and loyal as Becca."

My lips tilt into a smile. "Thanks, man. You might be right. But honestly, I'm fine. I know that

I have is the real thing. I don't need to defend it to anyone."

Asher nods. "Cool. Just wanted to check on you. You got kind of quiet after dinner."

I tilt my chin. "I'm straight. I promise."

"You feeling good for tomorrow's game?" he asks.

I nod. "Hell yeah."

"Alright, well," he rises to his feet once again, "I won't keep you up. Have a good night."

"You too," I say, watching him walk toward the door.

Once I'm alone again, I sprawl out across the bed and re-read the letter to myself, erasing bits and pieces here and there to fix my grammar as I go. And then I pick up where I left off.

One day soon I'm going to make you my wife, angel. And I can't freaking wait, and not just because our wedding night is going to be epic. (Though it totally is for the record.)

I have a brief but vivid mental image that pops into my head.... spelling out the word *Anal* with a question mark in red rose petals across a fluffy white bed. Not a bad idea… Although I'm not sure how romantic it is. Shaking the thought away, I keep writing.

I love you so much. I'll do anything in the world to honor and protect you. Thank you for trusting me with your heart. I love you, angel.

Owen

CROSSING THE LINE

Suddenly it doesn't matter that we're in my teammate Landon's living room with him sleeping mere feet away. Because the second Bailey dropped to her knees between my feet, all common sense flew out the window and it was game-over for my libido. I've wanted her all night.

Bailey doesn't waste any time undoing the front of my pants or slipping her fingers beneath the elastic of my boxers to draw out my aching cock.

"Baby," I groan as she strokes me from base to tip. "You sure about this?"

With a tender kiss to the swollen head of my cock, Bailey gives an eager nod. "Very sure."

And with a look that says *I want this in my mouth*, Bailey gets to work.

I curl my hands into fists and watch, helpless, as my sexy as fuck girlfriend proceeds to give me the hottest b-job of my life.

Her right hand, curled around me moves in time with her mouth. And her mouth… good God. It's hot and wet and the suction feels incredible.

A desperate noise escapes me and Bailey looks up, meeting my eyes with a look of warning.

"Sorry," I mouth.

With a deep inhale, I try to control my breathing, try to control the way my hips are lifting up off the couch to fuck her mouth, but I can't control anything. I can't last ... not like this. And after a few more pleasure-filled moments of Bailey sucking on me like a lolli-pop, I groan.

"Gonna come, baby."

She strokes and sucks until I erupt, swallowing me down like a damn pro.

I lean forward to kiss her forehead as Bailey grins up at me. "You're so, *so* good at that," I tell her. She chuckles.

A noise in the kitchen captures our attention. The faucet is running. What the hell? Quickly tucking myself back into my boxers, I help Bailey up off the floor.

"For the record, I didn't see anything," Landon says, waving a hand in our direction as he strolls from the kitchen back toward his bedroom.

"Thank fuck," I mutter under my breath.

"Well maybe I saw one little thing. Nice dick, Asher," he snickers.

Which sends Bailey into a fit of laughter.

I tug up my pants the rest of the way and rise to my feet. "We're leaving now," I say loudly to no one in particular.

• • •

Thank you so much for reading! To find out what I have coming up next, make sure you sign up to receive my emails here plus get 2 free books: **www.kendallryanbooks.com/newsletter**

Follow Kendall

Website

www.kendallryanbooks.com

Facebook

www.facebook.com/kendallryanbooks

Twitter

www.twitter.com/kendallryan1

Instagram

www.instagram.com/kendallryan1

Newsletter

www.kendallryanbooks.com/newsletter

Other Books by Kendall Ryan

Unravel Me

Filthy Beautiful Lies Series

The Room Mate

The Play Mate

The House Mate

Screwed

The Fix Up

Dirty Little Secret

xo, Zach

Baby Daddy

Tempting Little Tease

Bro Code

Love Machine

Flirting with Forever

Dear Jane

Only for Tonight

Boyfriend for Hire

The Two-Week Arrangement

Seven Nights of Sin

Playing for Keeps

All the Way

Trying to Score

Crossing the Line

The Bedroom Experiment

Down and Dirty

Crossing the Line

Wild for You

Taking His Shot

How to Date a Younger Man

Penthouse Prince

The Boyfriend Effect

My Brother's Roommate

The Stud Next Door

The Rebel

The Rival

The Rookie

The Rebound

For a complete list of Kendall's books, visit:
www.kendallryanbooks.com/all-books/

www.ingramcontent.com/pod-product-compliance
Lightning Source LLC
Chambersburg PA
CBHW031333060726
47590CB00007B/2450